The Banished

BY BETTY LEVIN

Greenwillow Books, New York

The text of this book is set in Fournier 285.
Printed in the United States of America
First Edition   10 9 8 7 6 5 4 3 2 1

Library of Congress Cataloging-in-Publication Data
Levin, Betty.
The banished / by Betty Levin.
p.   cm.
Summary: Siri, her uncle, and the Furfolk make a
perilous journey across the sea to deliver an ice
bear to the king as ransom for his lifting the
banishment which his grandfather had
imposed upon the people of Starkland.
ISBN 0-688-16602-4
[1. Fantasy.   2 Polar bear—Fiction.]   I. Title.
PZ7.L5783Ban   1999   [Fic]—dc21
98-39889   CIP   AC

For all—near and far, past and present—

who gather each year to become

Children's Literature New England

The Banished

1

"Grandmother, tell me about trees."

Grandmother glanced at Siri and sighed. "Isn't there enough to fill your head just now? We have ice bears and Furfolk at our doorstep, and you wish me to speak of trees?"

Siri gazed up at the bare branch that her great-great-grandparents had brought from their island home across the sea. No matter how sorely her family had needed wood, that branch had never been cut and used. Here in the Land of the White Falcons, where there were no forests, no houses of wood and thatch, no vast, fragrant meadows, it still hung above the door where it had been placed more than seventy years before.

Even though Grandmother was the last person in the Starkland settlement to hold in her mind's eye a true picture of the island from which they had been banished, the branch reminded all of them of their ancestral home. Everyone could almost see the ample island colored by changing seasons: deep green forests in late winter, the bright spring green of fields shot with yellow broom, the purple of heather on summer moorlands, and in fall the golden barley before harvest.

"I've seen the ice bear," Siri told Grandmother. "I've seen the Furfolk." The Starkland settlers were supposed to keep their distance from the bears and the Furfolk. But nothing like them had ever before so stirred the people, at least not within Siri's memory. Not that her memory held much. She would have to wait until she was as old as Grandmother to possess a lifetime of stories and marvelous events.

"Thorvald will return soon, he and the Furfolk man," Grandmother said to Siri. "There is always a crowd to watch the she-bear when they give her a seal. If you run now, you may find a spot where you can see."

Siri understood that she was being ordered to leave her grandmother in peace.

By the time her eyes adjusted to the dazzling whiteness outside, people were drifting down to the fjord. Someone must have spotted the skin boat threading its way among the ice floes, returning with meat. The Furfolk man had a magic way with seals and fish that no one in the village, except maybe Uncle Thorvald, could match.

Siri was proud of her uncle even though the respect he was afforded never seemed to include her. Surely respect ought to be cast from a man like his shadow. But however close she stuck to him, any attention paid to her held not one hint of respect. "Move, little gnat," she would be told, "before you get slapped." Or, "There, useless fish scale, be gone lest you be scraped off."

Just the other day Siri had complained about this treatment. "What is the good of Uncle's respect if he won't share it with his family?" she had demanded.

"Respect must be earned," Grandmother had told her.

As far as Siri could tell, that meant being obedient and

holding her tongue. Siri did well at some things like fishing and tending sheep. But obedience and silence did not come readily to her. What was the use of an opinion if you didn't air it?

"How did Uncle earn his?" she had asked.

"You know quite well. Not only is he the finest hunter in the settlement, but he is the only one to master the Furfolk language. If he gains freedom for all the men and women and children of Starkland, he will be the hero of our people. But the path to that end is as slippery as the ice that melts at midday and freezes smooth at night. The Furfolk man will not be hurried. Since our Elders grow impatient, we are fortunate that Thorvald understands Furfolk ways as well as their language."

Siri suspected that her uncle made up some of what the Furfolk said, to have his way. But when she said as much to Grandmother, she was sent outside to stand in the snow and think about her insolence. What she thought about, though, was her stupidity in voicing any thought to Grandmother that contained even a whisper of doubt about her beloved Thorvald.

That was the trouble with speaking your mind. It could land you in the snow when you fancied a place by the fire, close to the bubbling fish stew. Siri couldn't help thinking that a mother or an older sister would have taught her how to be clever enough to avoid being kept from the hearth.

It always came down to that. She envied children with mothers or sisters to show them how to pick their way around the vanities and tempers that could flare up at a single careless word. A clever girl would have shared her thoughts about Uncle Thorvald with someone who did not take offense. Next time she would speak only to Bran the dog.

"Siri!" shouted Gudrun, pelting headlong down the steep slope to the fjord. "Hurry, or you'll miss the kill."

Siri shook her head. If there was to be a kill, that meant Thorvald was bringing home a live seal.

"The Furfolk children will be fed, too," Gudrun called out, her long braids flying as she ran. "Don't you want to see them?"

But Siri did not. Something about those children made her stomach swim as it sometimes did when she fished from a boat in choppy water. She had seen them seize strips of raw flesh from their father's knife, had seen them fling themselves aside like dogs gnawing and gulping prey before it could be snatched from them.

Almost everyone in the settlement believed the Furfolk to be part human, part beast. Animals were simply animals. Siri understood them, even the thin she-bear, bound and terrified as she clutched her tiny cubs. But the Furfolk children were too much like—well, like Siri herself, like Gudrun and the others.

Yet the Furfolk mother was more like the she-bear than any human mother Siri had ever seen. Her lumbering body and her bearlike snuffles and grunts made her seem all beast. Bear talk, Siri supposed. That was how the Furfolk man calmed the snarling ice bear. They spoke the same language.

Siri wandered along the path that led uphill from the settlement. She heard a roar that started out sounding like the bear but became the voices of the people swelling with excitement. They were thrilled to have the savage beast in their midst, some because this ice bear might end their banishment, others because the sheer danger of her was so fascinating.

Not only were captive ice bears extremely rare, but kings across the sea regarded them as prized possessions. Long before Siri was born, the old king of Thyrne, craving one for his menagerie, had promised to lift the banishment imposed by his father if the people of Starkland delivered a living ice bear to him. The present king, his son, let it be known that he would honor that pledge.

Siri didn't turn back until the din settled into the ordinary gabble of many people talking at once. That meant the feeding was over.

Coming around the side of the stone sheep stable, she caught sight of the Furfolk children racing for the deep snow, where they threw themselves face forward as though diving into water. So that was how they dealt with all the slime that smeared their faces and their hooded tunics. If the Starkland children soiled their garments like that, they would get a swat across the head. Grandmother would make Siri scrub her shift and shirt until her knuckles were raw. But the bloodied Furfolk just rolled in the snowbank like puppies.

Now they rose, dabbing fistfuls of snow at each other's dark, round faces. Each was a mirror for the other. With identical fringes of black hair escaping beneath the fur-edged hoods, it was impossible to tell which was the brother and which the sister.

Siri shuddered. Sometimes Uncle Thorvald lived with these

creatures. If he hunted in the distant ice fields, the Furfolk man was his only companion for long, long stretches of time. Afterward he always seemed restless and morose and slow of speech. Then, when Furfolk words came unbidden to his tongue, it was almost as if some wild beast had taken possession of him.

2

"The Elders will be here tonight," Thorvald said to his mother. He gestured at Siri. "To speak of serious matters."

Grandmother nodded. "There will be no interruptions. Siri will be in her bed closet."

Siri opened her mouth to protest, to plead, but a glint in Uncle Thorvald's eye stopped the words before she could voice them. Well, she would not sleep. If she must shut herself away, she would listen to every word.

She looked at Grandmother, thin and bent, her joints grotesquely swollen. Even though she still kept at her spinning and weaving, the work came painfully to her. How could strong, tall Thorvald with his piercing blue eyes be her son? How could he be the brother of Siri's dead mother? Or rather, if he was Siri's true uncle, why was he so ready to ignore or dismiss her?

Grandmother came to Siri's bed closet to draw the curtain.

"I am shut inside when the sky is yet light," Siri complained.

"Tomorrow is another day," Grandmother told her. "Each new day is longer than the one before. The sun will not stay from her course because one child misses out on an evening's brightness."

"Why does Uncle care more for the Furfolk than for me?" Siri whispered.

Grandmother sighed. "The bears cannot be kept without the Furfolk man. It is only when the living she-bear is delivered to the king of Thyrne that the old king's promise will be fulfilled. Likely the present king cares little about our banishment, since it was long ago, when his grandfather's forays into distant lands brought his warships to our island for supplies. His men ate their fill and crammed all manner of goods into their ships, leaving the island all but ruined. When they stopped again the following year, the islanders resisted the seizing of their harvest, and so were banished. As you know, I was very young then, but my mother and father and grandparents suffered greatly, as did all the islanders. So the matter of the ice bear and the Furfolk affects every person in Starkland. Thorvald cannot risk the presence of a child who will not hold her tongue."

"I will," Siri retorted. "I just did."

Grandmother shook her head. "I blame myself for filling your mind with stories from the long-ago time when women and men, beasts and frost giants performed marvelous deeds. Since I may grow forgetful like the eldest Elder, it is necessary that you practice the tellings. Yet sometimes you fancy yourself a long-ago hero and forget you are a mere child. Besides, Thorvald thinks I have given you too much voice."

Siri knew that most Starkland women blamed Grandmother for Siri's boldness. They likened Siri to the tough willow scrub that clings to the shallow soil and pushes out the sparse, precious grass. Sometimes the women uttered dire warnings about her, how she would grow twisted and ugly. Wasn't it already unlucky, they said, that Siri was the only person in Starkland with hair as black as the hair of Furfolk?

"Why are the Elders coming here?" Siri asked, trying to keep Grandmother with her a little longer.

"Decisions must be made," Grandmother said. "When the first trading ship arrives from Thyrne, we must be prepared to send the bears across the sea. No trader will want to take on a she-bear with cubs, not after the last ice bear on a ship ended up killing two men. It had to be killed to spare other lives on board. This time, with the Furfolk man as bearkeeper, the delivery may safely be made. But it will cost Starkland a great deal, and the Elders need assurance that it will not be in vain."

"Will the eldest Elder be here?" Siri wanted to know. What she really meant to ask was how someone as addled as he could make any sensible decision.

"All three will be here," Grandmother replied. "And, Siri, do not mock the old one. There was a time when he figured greatly in the life of this settlement. Indeed, when he was young and strong, he captured a fine young ice bear, bigger and better than the one we hold now."

"What happened to that bear?" Siri asked.

"It had to be bound, of course. It strangled itself fighting to break free."

"So it was worthless?"

"It is said in Thyrne and everywhere else that, while a living ice bear is worth a king's ransom, a dead one is worth only the price of its fur. But there is more at stake for all of us here. The ice bear is our ransom."

"Then the decision is already made," Siri said.

"Maybe not. It is more complicated than I have said. The Furfolk woman's time draws near."

Siri sat up. "Time for what?"

"She will give birth soon. No one knows just when. Thorvald fears that if the man takes her away to her people just before the trading ship arrives, there may be no way to finish what is begun."

Siri was unable to keep Grandmother any longer because the first of the Elders could be heard at the door.

"Hush now," Grandmother warned. "Not another word."

Siri drew the coverlet up to her chin and stared at nothing. She knew every inch of the stones that closed her in. Not long ago, when Grandmother feared that fuel would not last the winter, Siri had practically lived in her bed closet, with Bran beside her for warmth. In the brief spells of dim daylight she had studied the crevices of her closet walls and imagined that they pictured the faraway landscape Grandmother sometimes spoke of—not the forest but the gentle grasslands that fed so many cows and sheep and horses that the eye could take in only a portion of it.

In Starkland, if you climbed to the summer willow scrub, your glance swept everything: the drying racks draped with fish on the rocks along the fjord, the low stone buildings housing people and their meager stock, and above the settlement the scant margin of grassland that had to provide winter hay as well as summer grazing.

Beyond the life-giving turf the willow leaves became fodder and the stems were cut for sticks with armfuls of uses. Even the bark was scraped for tanning and for the brew that eased aching bones. Where the rocky soil failed to hold the willow, nothing remained but bare stone or snow. Then you knew you had seen all this world had to offer, except for the never-ending ice.

Siri heard the Elders murmuring thanks and knew that Grandmother must be handing out mugs of sour milk for refreshment.

"The question is not only how many able men we can spare," said one Elder. "It is how we can persuade some traders to let our men take their places for this journey."

"Why should they trust us any more than we trust them?" said another. "They will rightly call for equal numbers, matching their men to ours."

"And demand much of our goods in payment," replied the first. "Can we afford to lose the bounty of a winter's hunting if we must also lose farmers and fishermen for half the summer?"

Grandmother spoke up. "And what if there is some mishap and the ship needs repair? If you do not return this summer," she warned, "you will leave us without our best hunters."

Siri wondered why no one objected when Grandmother interrupted. Was she an Elder, too, just because she was old? Siri let out an impatient sigh. Must she wait until her ideas had grown stale inside her head before she could make them known?

"When we return," Thorvald replied, "we will be laden with goods for living and trading. Remember, besides the she-bear, we will be rewarded for the two cubs."

"Is there any doubt, then?" asked the eldest Elder. "Is there disagreement?"

One of the others said to him, "Thorvald fears that if the Furfolk woman is gone when the ship comes, the man will refuse to leave. But I have heard that Furfolk do not become attached to one another as we do. That is why they have no names."

Thorvald said, "They do have names, but they are secret. To give them out is to give up their selves. And despite what you may have heard, the Furfolk man will not abandon his family. I assure you this is so."

"He can be compelled," said the eldest Elder. "He can be forced."

"And provoke other Furfolk to anger?" demanded another. "They would surely hear of it."

"Then if the man is truly attached to his family, Thorvald must persuade him accordingly," said the first Elder. "Let the children be held, not through force, but with Thorvald imposing some requirement he invents for the purpose. We need them with the Furfolk man on the journey."

"That may not be possible," Thorvald said in an undertone. "Furfolk customs do not change. They have no reason to yield to our laws, invented or otherwise."

"It is the only way," the first Elder told him. "We have to rely on the Furfolk man to keep the bear alive and also to keep her from doing harm. If the woman goes, we must have the Furfolk children to give us a hold on the man. If we risk our livelihood in this endeavor, we should have that power over him, here and on the sea journey. And both children, Thorvald, so that if one dies, there is the other in reserve."

Thorvald did not respond. Siri could only imagine his scowl or gesture. It silenced the others. That, or else the Elder's pronouncement, seemed to bring the discussion to an abrupt close.

3

In the morning Uncle Thorvald was gone.

"Hunting," Grandmother said, her lips closing with such finality that Siri knew no further question would pry them open.

Siri managed to escape before being set at carding wool for Grandmother to spin. Almost without meaning to, she glanced downhill toward the bear. Since no gawking villagers were near, she made her way in that direction.

This was not the first time that Siri had come alone to see the bear and her cubs. She shunned them when the settlers gathered, since they hungered for some display of savagery. The bear had already killed one dog that some claimed had wandered foolishly within range of its deadly paw. Others said that the poor dog had been kicked and prodded into the bear pit. Uncle Thorvald, backed by the Elders, had forbidden any further baiting or teasing. Too much was at stake, not just the lives of animals and children but the bear itself and the cubs, so valuable alive, so far from thriving.

The air rose chill from the fjord, where icebergs seemed like frost giants breathing vapors of frozen air. Siri covered her nose and mouth with the ends of her head scarf. Then, abruptly, the bear smell wafted through the cold, a smell full of heat and something sour but unlike the reek of the sheep stable.

A stout rope made of braided walrus hide bound the she-bear by a hind leg. Since the cubs were too tiny to scale the steep walls of stone, they were free to clamber around within the confines of the pit. The moment Siri came to the edge of the pit, the bear signaled the cubs and drew them against her body, her massive forelegs tight around them. She always did this, her defensive reaction to any person approaching.

Siri, on her knees, crouched low. The bear gaped up at her, silent.

Siri looked away. Then she sat, dangling her legs, still with her gaze averted. When she finally allowed herself a quick glance, the bear had shut her gaping jaws. Siri turned aside again. She waited.

Then out of the corner of her eye she noticed that the cubs had been released. She felt suspended between the cold above and the animal heat below. She tried to recall what she had overheard about the bear. But all she really knew was that the ice bear had been a small cub when the Furfolk man had taken her from her dead mother and raised her. Even after she was full grown, the bear came and went like a family dog, like Bran. When she dug her den, the Furfolk man had guessed that in the spring cubs would be born beneath the snow. And here they were, these very cubs, held in a pit until they could be shipped to Thyrne.

It seemed an eternity before one of the cubs tumbled within range of Siri's vision. With a thrill of understanding, she forced herself to shield her gaze from a full view of the pit. This might be the first time that the she-bear, in someone's presence, had not clutched her cubs to her. Even when she was tearing at seal or fish, she always kept her cubs pressed to the wall or inside the curve of her body.

Now the second cub pounced on the first, and the two rolled over and over in mock battle. The she-bear allowed this. She did not regard Siri as a threat. But what would happen if Siri moved?

Slowly she swiveled and then crawled from the edge of the pit. Slowly she rose to her feet. She longed to look back and down. Were the cubs still playing? Had the she-bear signaled them to return to her defensive posture?

Uncertain, Siri simply stood with her back to the pit and made herself stare at the empty snowpack. Only it wasn't empty. The two Furfolk children emerged on the level ground with what looked at first like a lump of the pack in motion. As they approached, they became hidden behind this giant snowball they had broken from the pack and were rolling toward the pit.

It was only when Siri stepped aside that the Furfolk children caught sight of her. Startled, they sought to reroute the snowball. But it was on a downward slope now, and there was no shifting it.

As soon as the huge ball of snow rolled over the edge of the pit, all three children ran to look. Siri forgot to be wary, to spare the she-bear the effect of her attention. But the Furfolk children, who were chattering and laughing, seemed to calm the bear. There was the snow, broken and spattered, and there were the cubs, rollicking in it, burrowing and swimming and flailing their legs.

For a moment Siri found herself laughing with the Furfolk

children. It was almost as if they had become human, like Gudrun or any other companion in play. The she-bear was stretching her forelegs, trying to scoop snow toward her. She licked up all she could reach, and then she stretched some more. But most of the snow was beyond her.

"She thirsts!" Siri exclaimed, her speech instantly silencing the Furfolk children. They looked at her as if only now aware that she was not one of them. Then they ran off in that strange wallowing gait that seemed even more beastlike from the rear.

"Bring more snow," Siri shouted after them. "The she-bear needs it."

But although she waited a long while, they did not return.

Allowing herself one final glance, Siri saw the she-bear grooming one of the cubs and lapping up snow that soaked the little one's fur. But that wasn't enough.

All the rest of the day, as Siri fed sheep and geese and then, finally, was trapped into carding wool, she kept seeing the bear stretching to reach the snow. Siri had noted the curving black claws embedded in the soiled fur. She knew that one fearsome paw could sever a person's head in a single blow. Yet she was stirred not to fear but to pity for that great beast. Pity and shame.

4

"When will Uncle Thorvald come?" Siri demanded. "The she-bear wants water."

"It is not for you to instruct your uncle," Grandmother retorted. But a moment later her voice softened as she told Siri that this hunt was to provide for the Furfolk woman. Meanwhile the children were to take snow to the bear pit.

"They did," Siri said. "But the she-bear could not reach most of it."

Grandmother sniffed. Then she said, "They will not be away for long."

But she was anxious. Twice a day she sent Siri out to search the horizon—first seaward to spot a trade ship heading for the mouth of the fjord and then inland over the ice-sealed fastness.

Siri exulted in these errands. Already she had come upon a few places shielded from the wind where melting had begun. When the sun shone most brightly, the slow drops from those rocky outcrops drilled through the frozen surface to expose sheltered patches of shale and sand. There tiny gray-green shoots appeared with sudden life and as quickly shriveled and blackened. Siri knew that when the time was right, a few thick-leafed plants would briefly bloom.

Once, tramping farther than usual, Siri glimpsed three black specks on the face of a white, jagged cliff. She waited to see if they drew closer, but they vanished in the distance. Afterward she could not be sure that what she had seen were Uncle Thorvald and the Furfolk man. Anyway, there had been three, not two, so it must not have been them.

It wasn't until the next morning that it occurred to her that if the Furfolk children were alone here at the edge of the village, the third speck might have been the Furfolk woman. When Siri mentioned what she had glimpsed, Grandmother looked troubled.

"You will bring the Furfolk children food," she told Siri as she wrapped four salt fish, stiff as boards, in a cloth.

"Why?" demanded Siri, who could only think of stained faces and blood-soaked clothing.

"Because it has been four days," Grandmother answered. "I thought Thorvald would have the man back here by now."

"Is the woman hunting with them?" Siri exclaimed.

Grandmother thrust the bundle at her. "Make haste," was all she said. "The children must be fed."

Siri had never before approached the Furfolk place by the snowbank where the skin boat propped on its side served as a windbreak. She thought of finding Gudrun to go with her. But Grandmother might catch a glimpse of her heading toward Gudrun's house. That was the wrong direction. That was not how to make haste.

So Siri set her back to the village, only to find that once again a giant snowball was rolling toward the bear pit. This time Siri was well above its path. She could see the two Furfolk children lean into the snow as they pushed it along.

They were not talking and laughing, just grunting as animals do that are forced to great labor.

Arriving at the pit ahead of them, Siri kept well away from its edge. The snowball had veered down the incline. Now the children had to push the great rounded lump of snow uphill. But it wouldn't budge for them. They gasped and grunted, and then one of them whimpered and sat down hard.

Siri dropped the bundle. Giving the pit a wide berth, she ran around and flung herself headlong at the snow. The whimpering Furfolk child clambered to its feet. Together the three of them heaved and pushed. At first nothing happened. Then they found a single rhythm that joined their strength, or their weakness, into something greater than any one of them.

The stubborn mound of snow slid sideways and then finally rolled just enough for them to renew their efforts. One more mighty shove, and the snowball tumbled over the edge. The three of them collapsed, each lying breathless on the snowy rock.

Siri was the first to sit up and look down. Even with the she-bear's hind leg tied, she could wallow in the snow as she gobbled it.

Siri ran to fetch the bundle for the children, but they made no move to take it. She opened the cloth to show them it was a gift of food. One of the children lunged toward it. The other blocked the eager gesture and then stiffly, with great reserve, received one fish. Both children eyed it hungrily. Then the one who held it tossed it down to the bear.

"No!" cried Siri.

Alarmed, the Furfolk children rose to their feet. Siri took

another fish, nibbled at it, nodded her head, and forced it on them. This fish followed the first one over the edge to the bear.

Siri saw that the she-bear had devoured both fish and was slurping snow. It paid no notice to the children at the edge of the pit. When Siri turned back to the Furfolk, they were gone.

It was easy for Siri in her coat-dress to catch up with them in their fur leggings and heavy tunics, but they would not stop. She followed them all the way to their place, which reeked from old blood and the bones of fish and birds. How could she keep the Furfolk from returning to the pit with these last salt fish? She recalled that the man handed strips of seal flesh to them on the point of his knife.

With the two of them eyeing her, Siri tore off a piece of the fish and thrust it at them. They exchanged guarded glances. Then the shorter child reached forward to receive the food and stuffed it into its mouth. Quickly Siri broke off a piece for the other child.

After that, all she had to do was break the remaining fish in half and dole it out at once to each of them. The shorter child choked on the larger piece, spit it into its small brown hands, and then shoved it in all over again. Watching this display of bad manners, Siri was struck by the pawlike shape of the hands.

When the fish was eaten, the children licked their fingers and then each other's faces. Like the bear cubs, Siri thought. After that they set their dark eyes on her. She couldn't tell whether they were conveying their thanks or pleading for more. Their gaze was direct, unwavering, mystifying.

The shorter of the two dropped to its knees and groped among scraps of sealskin before finding a bit with the fur rubbed off. It stuck this in its mouth and began to chew and suck, though whether to soften the skin or to gain some nourishment Siri could not tell.

Turning from their smelly place, she trudged back home to tell Grandmother that two of the salt fish had been fed to the she-bear.

"Well, and maybe it's just as well. How can that beast feed her cubs if she only gets a seal now and then?" Grandmother muttered. Then she asked, "Had they food, after all, the little savages? Is that why the two fish were given to the bear?"

"I think they are very hungry," Siri told her. "I think they have nothing to eat."

"Go search again, little minnow. Look for your uncle. I will think what can be done."

Siri was about to protest that she herself had not yet had a bite to eat this day. But she thought better of mentioning this. She would rather be sent out beyond the willow scrub than be kept inside to card wool.

Still, as she made her way toward the upland, she found herself licking her own fingers, just for the taste of the salt fish that lingered on them.

If only hunger could be assuaged with a lick.

5

Uncle Thorvald returned in the night. Siri would have slept through his homecoming but for Bran curled beside her. Even before Thorvald set foot on the step, the dog had bounded from Siri's bed closet and rushed to the door.

Grandmother padded forth in her sleep stockings while the dog still rumbled his soft growl of welcome.

"You were gone too long," Grandmother said. "The Elders came to inquire."

"They fear that the Furfolk man will desert us. So do I. It is harder for the Elders because they have no understanding of him. They have to put all their trust in me."

"I think that trust wears thin, my son."

"What am I to do?" Uncle Thorvald sounded weary. "The woman was restless. After we left her with her people, the man was so distressed that I could not understand all of what he said. For the sake of his family he would rather leave the bears and move on, although he says he is willing to make the journey with only the girl to help with the cubs if his son takes his place as hunter for the woman. I have not told him the Elders require both children. Knowing that the children might be used to force his continued service, I cannot contrive a sensible reason for him to bring them."

"Cannot someone else care for the woman?" Grandmother asked.

"Furfolk men and boys hunt for the women and children. That is their way."

"That boy cannot be much of a hunter," she exclaimed.

"He stands in for the man. There is the look of it."

"But the man returned here with you?"

"Yes. But the longer we wait for a ship, the more discontented he will grow. We will see whether his obligation to me is enough to hold him."

Siri couldn't keep silent, not when so many questions crowded her thoughts. Speaking from her bed closet, she said, "Why does the Furfolk man give up the bear and her cubs if they were his in the first instance?"

Grandmother and Uncle Thorvald, seated by the hearth, swung around to regard her.

"This child will be my undoing," Uncle Thorvald muttered.

"She is more grown than you realize," Grandmother said to him. "Let her know what you are about, at least in part. You may need her to know."

Thorvald beckoned to Siri, who slid down from the bed, dragging the coverlet with her, and scuttled over beside Grandmother. Thorvald placed his hands on his knees and leaned forward. "Are you grown enough to know when you must curl your tongue behind your teeth?"

Siri nodded. She could feel the heat from the fire creep up to her face.

"When our people were banished and sent here to make what living they could, many starved during the first winters.

More would have perished if Furfolk had not brought meat and taught them hunting skills. In time, without a common language, the Furfolk learned to use iron hooks and harpoon tips, which we supplied in exchange for furs and tusks. These we traded to seafarers, who brought us precious goods from Thyrne. All the while the people of Starkland and the Furfolk lived apart. The Furfolk left us the grassland for our livestock, and we left them the valley of the deep lake and the snowdeer that winter there."

"Is that where the woman is now?" Siri asked him. "I think the children want to be with her."

"No doubt," replied her uncle. "But what I—we—are attempting goes far beyond the wishes of one or two children. The Elders think the wants of a few Furfolk must be disregarded for the greater good. They do not recognize any other view."

Puzzled over the role of the Elders, Siri said, "I thought the arrangement was between you and the man."

A look of irritation came over Thorvald as if he had reached some limit with her.

Grandmother said, "All the settlement is involved. It was not your uncle alone who built the pit and risked the bear so close to the village. Nor could he or any other single person arrange to deliver her to the king of Thyrne. It is a hardship for everyone to hold back trade goods to make room for the bear and her cubs."

"Naturally all in Starkland will benefit if we deliver the bear alive," Thorvald added. "For the first time since our grandparents and great-grandparents were banished, we will be free to possess the land we inhabit, we will be allowed to carry and use weapons of war, and we will be free to travel where we will, even to live in Thyrne, as our earliest settlers once longed to do. The Elders know we have much to lose as well as much to gain." He was speaking to his mother now, not to Siri. "To the Elders the Furfolk man is like the bear, needed but not to be trusted. They see me as the one on whom they must depend to control the man who controls the bear. It is an uneasy alliance."

"Then give it up," Grandmother implored him.

"You know what that would mean?" he asked, startled.

She said, "When I was a young woman, I still dreamed of returning to my birthplace. But the time for that is past. I was proud to think that you would be our people's hero. Now I wonder whether the end of our banishment may bring more trouble than it is worth."

After a moment he shook his head. "I have always believed, as we all do, in the greater good. Still, I would be tempted to give up this effort. Only the Elders would not let that happen. You have just told me how anxious they were over my absence. They mean to see the thing through."

Siri wondered how the Elders intended to use the children to hold the man. Would they threaten to harm them, to carry them off? She nearly blurted out this question, but with her uncle and her grandmother head to head, this was the time to show them she could curl her tongue behind her teeth.

After returning to her bed closet, she mulled over what she could not ask. How could a good thing—the ice bear—cause so much trouble? Maybe, after all, it wasn't so good. An ice bear on its own was feared and respected. Captured, it might bring undreamed-of treasures and the greatest treasure of all, the end of banishment. But what of all its entangled connections?

She tried to separate the twisted strands of the past that bound the ice bear to Starkland's future as tightly as the leg rope of walrus hide held it captive. Some years ago, when the Furfolk man had killed its mother, he had spared the cub and raised it like a dog. Uncle Thorvald said that, as it grew, it came and went at will and showed no savagery toward its Furfolk family. Why had the Furfolk man raised the ice bear? Had the tiny beast charmed him the way a puppy burrows into a family's affections? How did he regard her now that she was grown and had cubs of her own? Did he understand the plan to present her to the king of Thyrne, far from the Land of the White Falcons?

Sleepily Siri's thoughts returned to the Elders. Had they some trickery in mind? Did her uncle suspect that the Furfolk were safe only as long as they were needed? If he did care what befell those fur-clad children, was it for their sake, for their father's, or for the survival of the ice bear?

Siri listened to Grandmother's murmur and Thorvald's flat response. She wondered how long it would be before Thorvald allowed her to join with them again, to speak and to be heard as if her ideas mattered.

Curling up under the coverlet, she drifted into silence.

6

The next morning Grandmother had to wake Siri. It was a fine day. The sheep could be let out, and the barn cleaned. This was a task that would take days to complete.

Siri stretched and yawned. "Must we begin today?" she asked.

"Thorvald may leave soon," Grandmother reminded her. "We should get on with it while he can still help with the heaviest work."

But Siri knew that she was the "we" Grandmother spoke of. Gudrun had a sister and a brother to help with the spring cleanup. Siri had no one. "It wouldn't be so hard if I had a sister," she muttered.

"Be careful what you wish for," Grandmother told her. "A wish may trip you up."

What did Grandmother mean by that? If Uncle Thorvald married, it would take some time for his wife to produce a baby. "Anyway," Siri declared, completing that thought, "a baby would be no help at all. A baby makes more work."

Grandmother cast a sidelong glance her way but made no comment.

Nettled, Siri tried once more to prompt her grandmother into revealing what was behind the warning. "How will the

Furfolk children fare on the sea voyage?" she asked. It was hard enough to picture the she-bear and her cubs confined for so many days. Bears and Furfolk on the open water?

But Grandmother turned away to ladle out gruel for Siri's morning meal.

Later, her feet and legs wrapped in coarse sacking, Siri spread precious hay on a patch of clean snow. After many months crowded into the dark stable, the sheep blinked and shook themselves, bedazzled. They sniffed the air, then tried to retreat.

Siri set Bran in the doorway. The sheep bunched together, all heads turned shoreward, ears flicking, nostrils trembling. They had picked up the bear scent.

With a handful of hay Siri tried to lure them away from the stone building that had kept them safe all winter. In the end they simply overran the dog and packed themselves back inside.

Defeated, Siri returned to the house. Grandmother was not there. But Siri had a plan. If the sheep feared the bear smell, probably they would fear the Furfolk as well. She would bring some salt fish to the Furfolk children and then get them to come with her. All she had to do was place them at the back of the stable to make the sheep flee. Maybe she could even persuade the children to guard the doorway in place of the dog.

Siri reached up and pulled from the line two salt fish. With one in each hand, she tried to run to the Furfolk place, but her wrapped feet and legs made her clumsy and slow. When she finally reached the propped skin boat and discovered behind it not only the children and man but Thorvald as well, it was too late to escape. Gesturing, the fish flapping in her hands as she pointed, she tried to explain to him what she was about.

"Did you think they would be hungry enough to obey your command?" Thorvald asked her.

"They were hungry before," she replied. "Besides, the man does your bidding, so why shouldn't the children do mine?"

"It is not the same," Thorvald told her. Then he added, "I have fed them already. Still, I think they may go with you. The man and I need to speak alone." Drawing the man aside, Thorvald conferred with him in the Furfolk language, so there was no use trying to hear what they said. Siri couldn't tell whether the children were curious enough to listen in. Their expressions gave nothing away.

Then the man directed his strange words at the children. It was clear to Siri that they understood they were to follow her. Turning from their father, they regarded her with dark, attentive eyes. She held out the fish, but Thorvald brought the giving to a halt.

"Afterward," he instructed her. "It will be their payment."

The three children trudged uphill to the stable. The Furfolk were wide eyed and uneasy as they approached the stone building. When Siri set the fish on the low roof that could be reached from the uphill side, the children seemed puzzled. They were troubled when Siri indicated that they must enter the stable with her.

The sheep uttered nervous snorts and backed as far as they could against the stone. The Furfolk children crouched down and went still. That seemed to quiet the sheep. Siri tried to show the children what needed to be done, but it was too dark inside, and the only way she could demonstrate was to lead them, forcing a way through the packed flock.

But the sheep would not budge. In the end Siri had to haul herself onto the backs of the sheep and crawl from one to another to get behind them. As soon as the Furfolk children followed, the forward sheep panicked and scooted out into the sunshine. That started a small stampede that dumped the Furfolk in the bedding. There they lay, laughing with relief and rubbing strands of wool between their brown, stubby fingers.

Siri laughed, too, but she did not join them on the dank bedding. She knew how quickly it could leave its reek on skin and clothing. Instead, she lifted the manure basket from its wall peg and dropped it in the doorway. Then, with a quick glance to make sure the sheep were busy at their scattered hay, she began to fork the upper layer of bedding into the basket.

After a while the Furfolk children sidled along the wall to watch. Clearly her actions puzzled them. She explained the process as she forked. Almost without her realizing what she was doing, this explanation led to a promise to give them a turn.

Did they understand? Probably not, even though one of them mimicked a few words. Did they guess her intent? She doubted it. But when the basket was heaped with bedding, she nodded to the Furfolk as she began to pull it away from the stable. At once they stepped in to help. One seized the forward edge of the basket, the other pushed from behind. Away and a bit downhill from all the village buildings they came to a depression in the slope where all the village dumped its refuse. Here Siri stopped and tipped out the contents of the basket, which she then dragged back to the stable.

Now the Furfolk children seemed even more bewildered. What would they think when all the rotting stuff from that dump was spread across the shallow soil above the village? Never mind, thought Siri. By then they would be on their way with the bears.

All morning she dug out bedding, resting when the Furfolk children dragged the full basket away for her. After a few cycles, they all three rested awhile. Suddenly she remembered about the fish on the roof. But they were gone. Either Bran had taken them or a raven had swooped down while no one was looking. How was she to reward the Furfolk? What would happen if she didn't? She still had days of cleaning ahead. Would they come again like this if they went away hungry?

The remaining bedding exposed to the air filled her nostrils with its acrid stench and made the Furfolk sneeze.

When Gudrun's brother stopped to gape at them, his only reaction was pity for Siri because of the oppressive smell, which he assumed came from the Furfolk children. "Worse than the bears," he remarked.

Already hot and thirsty and hungry, now Siri was embarrassed as well. "Say what you like," she shot back at him, "they are as strong and willing as any beast of burden."

That brought Gudrun's brother up short. "How do you instruct them?" he asked.

Siri couldn't keep from boasting. "I am learning bear talk. That is how the Furfolk man controls the she-bear. My uncle

says she was never tied until now. When they dug her out
of her snow den, before she and the cubs were ready, at first
she was too groggy to recognize the Furfolk. Also, she was
hungry from sleeping all winter. She will grow tame again
when the cubs are older."

"Still," Gudrun's brother declared, "I am glad I am not
her keeper when they carry her across the sea. It may take a
long, hungry time."

"Maybe the ship that takes her to Thyrne will be magic
and fly there," she said.

"A ship on the wing, Siri? That is one of your fancies."

"That shows how little you know," she told him. "In long-
ago times gnomes built a flying ship that could fold up small
enough to fit in a pack, yet was big enough to carry hordes
of people."

Gudrun's brother laughed. "You and your stories! Save
them for my little sister."

Siri couldn't think of another response, so she turned from
him and commanded Bran to close the sheep back inside. But
when she led the children home with her and they balked at
the doorstep, they were not so obedient as the dog. It was a
good thing Gudrun's brother couldn't hear her scream at
them, "I will give you fish and milk. You come inside and
be grateful."

Pressing close to each other, they stood as if planted on
the spot.

Grandmother opened the door. "What commotion is this?"
she demanded.

When Siri tried to explain, Grandmother remarked quietly,

"Likely they have been forbidden to enter any village house. It is enough that they braved the stable this day. Come and fetch some fish for them and send them on their way."

Siri started for the door.

Grandmother stopped her. "First unbind your legs. Are you no better than these Furfolk children in their hard-used tunics?"

Stung by this coupling of herself with the Furfolk, Siri unwrapped the sacking and tramped inside for the fish. When she returned, Grandmother was peering closely at the children. She had pushed back the hoods to reveal heads of hair as black as ravens' wings, but dull with filth.

"These two want care," Grandmother muttered as the children gnawed the fish.

Siri had to lead them most of the way back to their place. She might have resorted to sweeping gestures or even to kicking at them to show that she was done with them for now. But she had a plan to nurture. So she was mild and friendly as she walked with them.

When at last they saw that they were being dismissed, she smiled and waved them on and called out, even though her words could mean nothing to them, that she would be back for them the next morning.

7

That evening Uncle Thorvald mentioned that he and the Furfolk man would hunt seal the next day. Siri quickly asked for the use of the Furfolk children again. When Thorvald nodded, she could hardly contain her delight. Grandmother scowled and muttered that they needed their mother.

"What about me?" Siri demanded. "Haven't I gone motherless all my life?"

"You have had me," Grandmother reminded her. "You have been cared for."

Uncle Thorvald said, "They may not be without their mother for long."

Grandmother cast him a piercing glance.

"Unless a trading boat arrives soon, the man will not wait. His mind is on the woman." Thorvald lowered his voice. "I was wrong to tell the Elders so much. Now they know too well what the children mean to the man. As yet he has no sense of being ill used. If he did, he would take the children where none of us might follow."

"Maybe that is what should happen," Grandmother said.

"And lose the bears? After all this, lose them?"

"Would the man take the bears as well?" Siri asked. "How would he do that? May I watch?"

"Hush," Grandmother told her. "This is a grave matter."

"I know it is," Siri said, "but—" Her grandmother's glare silenced her.

"Even if I tell him why I am uneasy," Thorvald continued, "he may not comprehend. The Furfolk are not like us. How can the man learn to be devious?"

"Perhaps," said Grandmother, "you will have to be devious for him. But you must not betray his trust."

"I already have," Thorvald whispered. "I did not mean to. At the outset it seemed such a good idea. But now each time I talk with the Elders, I betray him."

Grandmother grabbed Siri by the shoulders and drew her close. "Not a word of this talk," she commanded fiercely.

Siri nodded. Never before had her grandmother spoken so harshly.

In the morning Siri was up in time to see her uncle and the man carry the skin boat over their heads to the launching slide. The Furfolk children came to her soon after, and the three of them took turns with the digging and hauling. They worked even longer than they had the day before because Siri knew she was about to lose them. If a trade ship came, they would be away from Starkland. If it didn't come and if the man heeded Thorvald's warning, they would go far inland. Either way, this stable-cleaning arrangement couldn't last.

It was midafternoon before the skin boat reappeared. Even at a distance Siri could tell that it rode low in the water. That meant it carried more than one seal.

When villagers began to descend the slope to the bear pit, Siri let the Furfolk go, too. Maybe seal meat would make them forget that she had not rewarded them this day.

She busied herself in the stable, using dried seaweed to cover the dank floor. She would collect some more from the rocks at low tide, but not yet, not now. She would not go near the shore while the bloody spectacle was in progress.

She was still with the sheep when she heard people hurrying back up the hill. Hurrying? What was the rush?

"Did the she-bear break loose?" she called to settlers running past.

"The trading boat," gasped one woman. "Your uncle caught sight of it."

"Where?" Siri asked. "How close?"

But the woman was out of earshot, and the others racing to make ready were too excited to stop for her.

Siri hurried home. This time Grandmother made her do more than unwrap the sacking before being allowed to join the throng that gathered on the rocks. Siri had to remove her dress and shift and wash herself and comb her hair. Only then was she given fresh clothing topped with the new cap that Grandmother had just finished. Its cloth was a fine springy weave, light and yet warm. Grandmother intended to attach it to a matching coat-dress that was not yet ready, but she let Siri wear the cap now to celebrate the arrival of the laden ship.

Grandmother tied the ends of Siri's long black braids with bits of yarn trimmed from the loom.

"Everyone in Starkland is fair but me," Siri complained.

"As you know, your father was a seafarer. Maybe he came from darker folk. When his ship was damaged and he had to overwinter here, he did not speak about his past."

"Was my mother— Did she mind how I turned out?"

Grandmother smiled. "As long as she had the strength, she held you. She thought you a wonder." Grandmother tweaked the cap, which tailed off down Siri's back. "Your mother vowed that you would have the longest braids of any girl in Starkland. And so you do."

"But they are black," Siri said with a frown.

"Yes," Grandmother agreed. "Very black."

Running outside, Siri tossed her head to feel the tail of her cap whipping with her braids. Catching sight of Gudrun, she called out to her and twirled around to show off the long tail. Gudrun admired it.

"You are so lucky, Siri, to be the only child." She raised her hands to her own cap, worn thin by her sister and brother before it had been passed on to her. "My mother means to trade most of her newly woven cloth for barley off the ship."

Siri made no response. She understood that the traders would be limited by what they could carry away with them in addition to the bears and meat to keep the she-bear alive. The traders were likely to choose fur and walrus hide and tusks before cloth, however fine. Gudrun's mother might have to wait for the next trade ship.

The two girls found a rock to perch on with a view down the fjord. Soon other children joined them, exulting in the rare freedom from chores at home. Siri suspected that Grandmother was not the only householder to prefer having no one underfoot while food was prepared for the feasting to come.

A shout from farther down the fjord alerted the settlement to the first sighting. Siri stood up. At first she saw nothing but swarming seabirds. Then from behind an ice floe emerged the top of the square sail, its pole pulled almost sideways. It shifted, and there was the ship, wallowing without direction, while men moved to drop the sail and to lash the pole to the gunwale before lowering the mast.

There was so much commotion on the vessel that only after the oars had been fitted and the final approach had begun could Siri count the eleven men. She wondered which families would play host to them. There would be cooking in every house.

Looking down into the ship, she could see that deep in its center was a pen full of animals. People standing near the children were either pleased because they needed a new bull or disappointed because they were were looking for timber or iron. Everyone had an opinion of some sort. They crowded down to help unload.

Siri wondered whether a pen that held one bull and several rams would hold a she-bear and her cubs. But she was thinking ahead. For now there were greetings, then food and drink to welcome eleven men eager to set foot on land, men longing to draw close to fires and to refresh themselves with hot water and clean garments. All this was expected. Common courtesy and custom established that they would be attended to before they set up their booths and spread out their goods. So it wasn't until later that Siri discovered what her uncle had learned at the moment of arrival. The ship had to be hauled and tarred before going to sea again. And a few seamen were reluctant to sail with an ice bear, the riskiest cargo imaginable.

In Grandmother's house Thorvald and the Elders grappled with the urgency of their cause. Two of the seafarers were loud of voice but bleary for want of sleep. Their leader, Grim, had a deep scar disfiguring his face and a severe limp. He intended to come again to Starkland this season and then to sail on in search of the vast timberlands beyond the western horizon. But first he would return to Thyrne to leave behind those in his crew who declined to sail in unknown seas. Others, eager for the adventure, would be gathering there, waiting to join him.

Like the threaded shuttle in Grandmother's loom, words shot between the lifts and pauses of conversation, weaving a pattern too piecemeal to be fully discerned. Yet positions were forged: the payment necessary to traders returning to Thyrne without the full portion of goods they had counted on; the determination to send a few Starkland men on this momentous journey with the bears.

When finally two of the Elders led the two seafarers off for the night, only Grim remained with Thorvald and one Elder. By now Siri, still fully clothed and too sleepy to draw the curtain, drowsed in her bed closet.

Thorvald invited those mariners who planned to sail west with Grim to stop in Starkland awhile and gather strength for the voyage. Starkland men could take up their oars, risking the danger of bears on the ship and working alongside those who chose to stay behind in Thyrne next time. Once the bears were delivered to the king, the new mariners awaiting Grim could take the places of the few who left the ship.

The plan took shape as fabric is woven, the cloth stretched and firm and intricately patterned. If it was like Grandmother's, thought Siri, not one thread would be out of place.

8

The next morning the animals were unloaded first, then the timber and iron, the grain and tar. Men and women from the outlying farms vied with villagers who had already laid claim to these goods that everyone needed.

With all the trading going on, it was easy for Siri to slip off to the Furfolk place. She had in mind finishing the stable cleaning. But the Furfolk children were nowhere to be found. Had the man seized this opportunity to whisk them away to safety? Was anyone else aware that they had vanished?

She scurried back to the house. Grandmother at her loom was so engrossed in her weaving that she didn't even glance up when Siri called for Uncle Thorvald.

"Siri," she declared, "you blow in here like a storm."

"But does he know the Furfolk are gone?"

Grandmother turned, the shuttle poised. "It is not a matter for you to consider," she said evenly.

"You mean, it is in Uncle's plan?"

Grandmother half rose from the bench, then changed her mind. The warp weights clinked together as she resumed her position. With a mighty thrust she sent the shuttle through the threads. "Run along, child," she said. "Leave me in peace."

Siri unwrapped her legs and wandered down to the water-front. A babble of voices issued from the trading booths. Finally she caught a glimpse of her uncle's tall figure. He was in a cluster of villagers, farmers, and fishermen. Several of them were speaking at once. Arguing? But they had known one another all their lives. What had them so riled now?

Siri moved closer. She skirted the group, hoping to catch her uncle's eye.

"How many men must you have?" asked young Modi from Outermost Farm.

"No less than five or six," Thorvald replied. "Five who know boats and are strong rowers."

"Even those of us who fish have little experience of the open sea. And it is the sail, not oars, that brought this ship over the sea so swiftly."

Thorvald spoke quietly. "The seafaring traders have sailing experience enough. We know we can rely on one another and on the Furfolk man, who will keep the bear on the voyage. We may have to wait until the king or an underking can receive her. But each man of Starkland will be assured that his family will not want in his absence."

"On whose word?" demanded another.

"The Elders have made this pledge."

As the men considered Thorvald's argument, voices dropped or trailed off. In this lull Siri pressed forward. "Uncle Thorvald," she called to him.

He shook his head and waved her away.

"But do you know they are gone?" she blurted.

Thorvald spun around, his face set. "Not now. Leave us."

"Gone?" demanded one of the men. "Who? What is she saying?"

"She speaks of household matters," Thorvald replied smoothly. To Siri he said, "No more. Wait for me in the stable. Go now."

Siri felt the sharp reprimand beneath this soft-spoken order. Uncle Thorvald should be glad of her vigilance. Instead, she was banished to the sheep for speaking out of place.

He was a long time coming. It was dark and dreary inside, and she minded missing all the activity along the shorefront. Eventually she heard the unmistakable chant of men pulling together. If they were hauling the ship, that must mean it was being readied for the voyage to Thyrne. Had the Furfolk been found, or would the plan go forward without them?

When Thorvald finally appeared, he was carrying a bundle over his shoulder. Without speaking to her, he hung the bundle in the dark recesses of the stable above the backs of the sheep. When that was done, he said, "You will remain here until dark. You will see no one. You will speak to no one."

She said, "Does Grandmother know I'm here?"

He said, "She knows what she must know." Then he left.

Siri guessed that Grandmother would think of her alone and hungry. Soon Grandmother would bring some cheese or fish to her.

After sliding down to the rockweed bedding, Siri leaned against the stone wall. One ewe came and pawed beside her, then folded its legs and sank down as close as it could. Siri dug her fingers into the long, thick wool. At least she wasn't cold here.

Closing her eyes, she tried to picture the trade ship climbing ashore. Many people would join in this effort. The timbers it rolled on must be kept straight, and there would be a crew with a fresh roller to insert as each one was left behind. Rollers that had been the stems of trees in far-off forests. Imagine trees as tall as that.

She was sound asleep when Uncle Thorvald returned. His manner was so bewildering that she could not follow his rapid, disconnected orders: Come outside. Be still. Stand. Follow.

In the darkness a loaded sled stood out from the snow. Grabbing the pulling rope, Thorvald set off. He set a swift pace, the only sound between them the glide of the sled runners. Bran ran ahead, then circled back to Siri. That was reassuring. Now that they were on their way, Uncle Thorvald paid no heed to her, but the dog would not let her fall behind.

At first she longed to know where they were heading. As time went on, she longed to know when they might stop and rest. She would have clung to the rear of the sled if she had dared. Didn't Uncle Thorvald realize that she had been without food all day? Did he think she could keep up like this all night?

They must have passed the Outermost Farm before Siri realized it. Now, as dawn streaked the sky, they traversed hunting land, the tongue of the glacier just visible in the distance.

When Uncle Thorvald stopped, Siri stumbled into the sled. The impact thrust her backward. She found herself sitting, dazed and stupid, unable to rise. Uncle Thorvald busied himself with the small pack he carried on his back. Then he threw something to the dog and stepped around the sled to hand Siri a strip of salt fish.

She was too exhausted to eat it, too thirsty. Bran came over to her, licked her face, and stole one taste of the fish without snatching it out of her hands. She grabbed him and buried her face in his neck. Her uncle's silence frightened her. She keeled over on her side and drew up her knees as she would in her bed closet. But her uncle nudged her and would not let her lie there.

"Eat snow," was all he said.

"I'm tired," she whimpered.

But he would not relent. They must be on their way.

The sun was high before they rested again. By then all she could see was the rear of the sled and the twin lines carved by the runners. She no longer wondered where he was taking her. If only she could lie still, she thought, closing her eyes.

He stood over her, but she couldn't see his face. Then he leaned down and raised her by the shoulders. He was speaking to her, but she was panting so hard that she heard only her own labored breaths. He lifted her and draped her, facedown, over the bundle on the sled.

"You must hold on," he told her.

Her fingers groped for the walrus-hide rope. But as soon as she began to give in to sleep, she let go and was dumped off. Thorvald didn't stop for her, so she ran to catch up and clambered back on. This time she wriggled her hands and one leg beneath the lashings, binding herself to the bundle.

At the next stop Uncle Thorvald ordered her back on her feet. He said he needed his own strength for a swift return.

"Return from where?" she finally asked.

He pointed, but she could see nothing ahead but snow and rock and the looming glacier. Then, her eyes adjusting to the brightness, she realized that some of the rocks on a distant ridge were moving, a long line of black specks winding upward and vanishing behind a near hill.

"Snowdeer?" she whispered.

He nodded. "They head for higher ground when the melting begins. Some Furfolk have already left the valley of the deep lake, too."

"Did the man go with them?" she asked.

"No, he is with the woman and their new child."

But that didn't really explain very much. What about the bears?

Uncle Thorvald leaned into the weight of the load and resumed hauling. Siri followed again, stiffly at first, and then gathering strength to keep up.

Now that Uncle Thorvald was speaking to her, she felt more hopeful. Even if this journey was a kind of punishment, it wouldn't last forever. What mattered now was that she keep from angering him further, and that meant holding back new questions until she knew the most important ones to ask.

On they went. The way seemed endless. Then, just as a haze began to filter the sunlight and Siri found the glare more bearable, Uncle Thorvald paused ahead of her and dropped the pulling rope. He stood there, staring at something. She struggled forward a few more paces.

Following the direction of his gaze, she looked down into a valley and its deep dark lake. Huts and drying racks were grouped on one side. She could see Furfolk moving about.

Now she thought she understood. Her uncle had come to fetch the man away for the sea journey. Only why had he brought her along?

Thorvald busied himself with the ropes until he had part of his bundle unwrapped. He removed knives and a broadaxe fresh from the trade ship. Telling Siri to stay, he tied the dog to the sled and set off on a track that hugged the steep hillside, descending gradually. He seemed unhurried and easy in his approach.

Siri wondered at this transformation. She knew how anxious he was, how pressed. But she also knew that he always took pains to study his quarry before approaching within striking distance. Did he expect the Furfolk to attack him? Even with a broadaxe and new knives, could he defend himself against so many of them?

Siri thought she could tell as soon as Thorvald was noticed, but she was too far away to recognize the man or his children. Anyway, the Furfolk all looked so much alike that she might not even tell close up which of them she knew. She watched as one Furfolk after another spoke with her uncle. Then one of them led Uncle Thorvald behind a drying rack. Siri held her breath for a moment. Maybe he would be ambushed and killed and she would be left there, stranded.

Thorvald was out of sight for so long that Siri finally sank down on the sled to rest. If he didn't return for her, she would need her strength to flee for her own life. Glancing back, she had no difficulty marking the footprints and runner lines in the snow. The haze, she now realized, hovered over the valley. Behind her, even in the pale light of evening, everything was clear.

She didn't see the two Furfolk draw near until they were almost upon her. Taking their silence for stealth, she considered trying to break away, but they were too close now. She was trapped.

Still, she fumbled in the pack, hoping to find another knife there, something she could flash before them, to hold them off. She was still rummaging in the pack when suddenly they were upon her. Looking up, she drew in a huge breath and then let out a gasp. They were only children, these two. They were her very own Furfolk.

She could have hugged them. But recalling her uncle's careful approach to the Furfolk, she forced herself to be restrained. She showed them that she was hungry, nothing more. They seemed to understand. They beckoned her to follow. They would not have come like this if anything bad had happened to Uncle Thorvald. He must have sent them for her. Anyhow, she had nothing to fear from them. After all, they were used to doing her bidding.

9

It was a long way down to the Furfolk. Near the encampment the trodden path was slippery. When Siri skidded, her feet coming out from under her, the children stopped, but without moving to help her up. This made her cross. They lacked courtesy. After all, she was a visitor in unfamiliar surroundings. With the light draining from the sky and the haze rising from the deep lake, it was hard to see where to step.

The Furfolk settlement consisted of huts banked by snow. They seemed to be made of skin stretched on curved poles. But when Siri drew closer, she saw that the poles were bones.

Suddenly a wall of children closed around her. They pointed, laughing. One took hold of her sleeve. Another went behind her and tugged at the tail of her new cap. Their smell was powerful, hinting of meat, making her empty stomach clench and her throat close.

Then a voice broke through the clamor. The children released her and stepped back. There was the man. After speaking to the children, he gave a curt nod at Siri and walked off. Uncertain, she just stood there.

Uncle Thorvald called to her from a hut some distance away. "Don't keep him waiting. There is little time."

Time for what? she wondered, scurrying to catch up with the man.

It was dark inside the hut. She looked around for food but couldn't see any. "Please, Uncle, I'm hungry," she whimpered.

"They will bring you meat," he told her. "As soon as I am on my way."

"On your way home? Without me?"

"The man will bring you. It is arranged."

"No!" she cried. "You can't leave me here."

"Hush. There is no other way. Behave in a fitting manner."

Siri clung to him. "Please, Uncle. I will behave. Only let me go home with you."

Thorvald detached himself from her. "Now listen," he said. "This concerns more than one girl who buzzes and whines like a swarm of ravening insects. I will explain this to you now and not again. Without the bears, we forfeit our chance to become free. Without the man, there is little hope of delivering the bears to the king. Now that the woman has given birth, the man will not leave without providing for her. He has agreed to come only if his son remains with her. But the Elders need assurance of the man's fidelity. And the two children are their surety."

Siri shook her head. She felt dizzy with hunger and confusion.

One of the Furfolk children handed something into the hut and went away. Siri saw that Thorvald was holding whatever it was. Since it didn't seem to be food, she paid no attention to it.

"So the son will stay behind?" she said, still trying to puzzle through what he seemed to be telling her.

"He will remain. That is what the man requires, what the Furfolk require."

"Why then must I stay?" Siri asked him.

"In two days' time the man will bring you back to us with the other, with the girl child. All Starkland will note the return and think they see the same pair of children as before."

"But I am not like them!" Siri blurted. "Nothing like."

Thorvald thrust what he was holding into her arms. "This is what you will wear. You will go straight to the Furfolk place and remain there with the Furfolk girl until we set sail. It will be done quickly. That is why you must stay here until the time is right."

Siri found that she was holding a heavy garment with some fur on it. "Wear this?" she gasped. "I can't. It's unclean. It's the skin of some animal."

"It is how you will dress until the truth may be revealed."

"Does Grandmother know?" Siri demanded.

"She knows I have taken you to the Furfolk and I have promised you will return. Remember, it was she who said to devise a scheme the man would not think of."

"But Grandmother never meant this," Siri told him, relief flooding through her. "She would never let me don such— such beastlike garments."

"Put them on," Thorvald ordered. "If it is ill-fitting, the Furfolk will find others. The man views you as a poor trade for his son, but he understands you were all I had to deal him. The trickery baffles him. Yet he trusts me. And I have said that there must be two Furfolk children on board with him and the bears."

"I have had nothing to eat," Siri complained. "I shall tell Grandmother how you treated me."

"It was my intention that you be hungry," Thorvald informed her. "Otherwise you would disdain the Furfolk meat as you disdain their skin garments."

Another child appeared in the opening to the hut. Thorvald went to receive what was brought and then sat himself down. Siri could hear him gnawing and chewing. Her stomach lurched and tumbled.

"Uncle," she pleaded, "have you no cheese with you?"

"There is meat here. Put on the leggings and tunic. Hand me your cloth garments that I may return with them to the village. Then I will share the meat."

She just sat there, overwhelmed.

"Haste now," he said, "or I shall depart without your clothing, and it will be left here. The Furfolk will soon move on and will be gone all summer. Do you wish them to carry off the things your grandmother wove for you?"

Siri struggled in the darkness. The leggings were so stiff that she drew them off and reclaimed her stockings and shift. At least that way the skin clothing would not chafe her skin. The tunic with attached hood smelled so rank as she pulled it over her head that she had to hold her breath. Feeling her cap slip down, she snatched it back and stuffed it inside one of the boots that she drew over the leggings.

Finally she gathered up her cloak and skirt and moved to the opening where her uncle sat eating.

He looked at her, nodded his approval, and sank his teeth into the meat. It looked raw.

She pressed her face into her woolen clothes and inhaled deeply.

"Put them into my pack," he ordered. Then, with his old knife, he cut off a strip of meat and offered it to her on the tip of the blade.

"What happened to the knives and axe you brought?" she asked him.

"Gifts," he replied. "Promises," he added. "If you are hungry, you will eat what is here."

"I am hungry," she answered, stifling a sob. She took the meat, smelled it, and let it fall. She shook her head.

Thorvald rose to his feet. "As you like," he told her. "When you are hungry enough, you will not refuse their food." He cut another strip and hung it on a snowdeer skull.

In the opening he faced her. "Do not shame me," he said. "Heed the man. Keep up your strength. If this scheme fails, let it be for other reasons, not for want of my wit and will— or yours."

With the remaining meat still in his fist, he hoisted his pack and set off.

Waddling to the opening, she watched him stride toward the path that led out of this valley. She almost called out. She would have run after him, but running was impossible in this heavy, stiff coating that imprisoned her.

10

The children brought more meat. One of them examined the strip Thorvald had left and shoved it toward Siri. She shook her head. "No," she told them, "it is bad. I cannot eat it."

After conferring, the taller one offered her the larger chunk they had brought. Siri burst into tears.

Hastily they backed away from her. Then they ran off.

Much later the shorter one reappeared, this time with a dried fish. Siri sniffed it cautiously, then bit into it. It tasted nothing like the salt fish she was used to, but it didn't turn her stomach.

When there was nothing left but bones and fins, she looked around for a refuse heap. The child led her outside and showed her where the bones could be left. After that the child led her farther and stopped at the edge of a smelly pit. Siri understood that this was where she was expected to relieve herself. She looked around, half expecting that wall of curious children to have lined up behind her. But no one else was near, so Siri made use of the place.

She tried to ask the child about water, but her washing gestures were met with a blank stare. Siri would have gone to the edge of the lake, but she was afraid to leave the child. "My name is Siri," she said, pointing to herself. "Siri," she repeated.

The Furfolk child pointed to itself in just the same way. "Siri," it said.

Siri's heart sank. She longed to have a name she could say, the name of someone who connected with her on terms she could understand. But the Furfolk child left her at the mouth of the hut and went off without a backward glance.

Siri told herself that the child had gone to be with the mother and the new baby. She told herself that someone would care that she was on her own here. She told herself that when Thorvald returned home, Grandmother would be frantic and furious. She would make him send for Siri at once. Grandmother would never agree to this scheme of disguise and danger. And abandonment.

For that was how Siri regarded herself. Abandoned. Thrown to the Furfolk. Her uncle had treated her brutally. He was like the villager who threw the old dog to the she-bear.

Siri waited and waited for at least one of the children to return. Finally exhaustion conquered her wariness, and she slumped down on a pile of skins.

She awoke to many sounds, many voices. Looking outside, she saw sleds being loaded, fish being packed. As she stood in the hut opening, two huts were dismantled, the supports lowered, the skin roofs and walls collapsing.

There was no sign of her Furfolk children, at least so far as she could tell. She had no idea which hut housed their

mother and the new baby. And there were children everywhere, all dressed alike in leggings and long coats with fur-
trimmed hoods.

By midday two heavily laden sleds had left the valley.
Dragging them looked backbreaking. Many people, large and
small, were hitched to the lines. No one, not one person, was
given a ride.

After this departure, quiet settled over the encampment.
Siri thought she heard an infant crying. She strained to hear
where the cry came from, but it quickly stopped.

Like the mist trapped in this valley, time held still, heavy
and oppressive, sealing the encampment from the vast white
world beyond. Only hunger kept Siri aware of the day's swelling and then shrinking into evening once more.

One child brought her fish. When they came singly, Siri
couldn't tell which was the shorter, which the taller. Maybe
this one would respond properly if Siri spoke her name again.
But the risk of being mimicked was too great. It was better
to say nothing, hear nothing, than to have her own name
reduced to an echo.

The second day passed even more slowly than the first.
Furfolk went away, but without sleds and packs. Siri supposed
they were hunting. No huts were dismantled. When children
passed nearby, they darted looks at Siri, but none approached.

When she caught sight of the man walking toward her, she
had to fight an impulse to back into the darkness. He carried
more skin garments, which he handed to her with a nod. She
guessed these were meant for her to put on, although they
looked much the same as those she wore.

In the darkened hut it was impossible to detect any difference. As she pulled off the boots she had been wearing, the cap she had hidden in one of them tumbled out. Glancing back at the waiting man, she tucked it inside the new boot. He didn't seem to have noticed anything amiss. He just waited to receive the garments her uncle had made her change into.

The new skin leggings and tunic were lighter and softer, the attached hood edged with long white fur. Could it be made from the pelt of a frost fox, a skin so precious that it was usually kept for trading? Inside there was a drawstring to close it tightly around her face.

This change lifted her spirits, and she smiled as she gave the man the stiffer garments. He spoke a word or two in his language, then tugged at her to come outside. There he prodded her into bending and reaching as he checked the tunic's length and width like Grandmother fitting her to a dress of woven cloth.

She stayed outside. After he left her, she ventured farther, passing close to some of the huts, but with never a glimpse into their dark interiors. From a distance she saw Furfolk working with bones and tusks, shaping points and drilling holes. Others kneaded snowdeer skin or sewed.

A small child in boots and tunic but no leggings stomped up to her and pulled from its mouth a length of whitened animal tendon it had been sucking. The little brown fist reached up to her, offering to share this morsel. In spite of her revulsion, Siri squatted down on her heels, cupped the fist in her hands, and pretended to take a turn with the stringy white stuff the child held out to her. The little one uttered a throaty chortle and stuck the tendon back into its own mouth.

One greasy finger stroked Siri's cheek, and bright dark eyes gazed into hers.

Then an older child grabbed the little one, spinning it away from any further contact with Siri.

Shocked, Siri stood up. Was she shunned out of respect or fear?

Slowly she made her way back to the hut, and this time she stayed inside. When she slept, she held her grandmother's cap to her face so that she would imagine herself at home in her own bed closet. But the dream that came to her was of a small brown hand stroking her cheek.

11

Siri awoke to a real brown hand shaking her shoulder. Even in the gloom of the hut she knew it must be one of her Furfolk children. She sat up and rubbed her eyes. The child leaning down to her was insistent; its hand still gripped her shoulder.

Siri nearly tripped over a bundle of tusks lying across the opening. Still half asleep, she visited the pit and then returned to the hut, where both children now awaited her. They gestured and prodded to show her that they wished to bind a pack to her back. She straightened, refusing to allow this. Did they think that she would toil for them because they had helped clean the stable?

"The people of Starkland do not work for Furfolk," she told them.

Of course they couldn't understand her words. Nor did they heed her lofty tone. One of them clamped hands at her waist, and the other slid a kind of harness over her head. The next thing she knew, the tusks were being hoisted onto her as though she were a beast of burden. Their weight dragged at her.

"But you are the beasts!" she cried, tears springing to her eyes. "If my grandmother saw this, you would be driven off to freeze on the ice."

The children spoke to each other without alarm or even concern. When Siri's pack was firmly in place, one of them knelt to receive the remaining tusks. This took longer because there was only one child to cinch the walrus-hide ropes and balance the load.

"This is too heavy," Siri told them. "Mine is heavier than that one," she claimed, although she had no way of knowing this. "You wrong me."

More words were exchanged between the two Furfolk children. Then the one with the pack trudged off toward the path. The other prodded Siri into taking one reluctant step, then another.

"I can't," she wailed, feeling herself shoved forward.

The child ahead of her didn't look back. The child behind her became more forceful.

Soon she found that it was easier to set her own pace than to move in response to being goaded from behind. As the path grew steeper, she put all her strength and energy into handling the incline and balancing the weight on her back. At length she stopped thinking about how sorely she was being treated. She simply kept going.

Although it was still very early in the day, the light on the snow made her eyes stream with tears. With her head bent, all she saw were magnified crystals that seemed to hold fire. The higher she climbed, the clearer the air became, and the more painful the blinding sun dazzle.

By the time the child ahead dropped to its knees, Siri was hot and dizzy and breathless. It was many moments before she was able to look around at her surroundings. The first thing she recognized was Uncle Thorvald's sled. It surprised her that he had left it.

She felt the pack dislodged from her back. Then the child backed up to Siri, who understood that she in turn was to unburden it. But Siri had trouble with the bindings and was still struggling to loosen them when she was nudged aside by the other child, who had arrived so silently that she hadn't realized it was there behind her.

Not only the second child but the man as well. He had dragged part of a walrus carcass all the way up here, while the second child had hauled a snowdeer haunch. The stench from this meat clogged Siri's nostrils and closed her throat. At the same time hunger pains cut into her, sudden and sharp. She doubled over.

One of the children raised her up and spoke to her in a kindly, though offhand, manner. It might have been telling her to cheer up, that the worst was over. But of course there was still the long trek ahead. Nothing was over. And even without the heavy tusks on her back, she would be unable to keep up without real food, without drink.

She watched the man lash the carcass and the tusks to the sled. Then he cut some meat from the haunch and doled it out to all three children. Siri saw that inside the blackened crust the meat looked almost fresh. She watched the Furfolk children chew on theirs. Cautiously she raised the cut end to her mouth and tasted. Closing her eyes, she nibbled. After the first swallow, she tore off one small mouthful after another until all that remained was the hard, foul rind, which she couldn't stomach. When she laid it down, the taller child reached for it, hesitated, until a nod from the man allowed the child to snatch up what she had rejected. After that the man beckoned to the child and held it in a long embrace. When he released it, the child turned, paused briefly beside the shorter one, and set off for the valley.

So that was the boy, Siri told herself. That was the son and brother taking his leave of them.

Except it was they who were leaving.

Siri hoped that there would be a rest time. But almost at once the man fitted himself into the pull ropes and lurched the sled forward.

Siri couldn't help noticing how subdued the shorter Furfolk child was as it stepped between the runner tracks. Not it, Siri realized. It no longer, this Furfolk child. She.

12

After the first few hours, the downward slope that spread before them was a welcome sight. But Siri's relief didn't last long. Wherever the sun had melted a little of the surface, the way was too slick for the heavily loaded sled, and the man needed help holding it back.

The Furfolk girl understood at once. She seemed to know almost beforehand when she must grab hold and dig her heels in. Siri tried to think of simple words that the man might understand, words to inform him that she was above such lowly toil. When she spoke to him, he merely shook his head, shook her off, his expression strained and distant. She had no way of telling whether he was troubled because of leaving his son and wife and baby or whether he simply overspent his strength with only two girl children to help.

In spite of her sense of being wronged, Siri bent to the task, following the Furfolk girl's lead and catching hold of the sled whenever it skidded and seemed about to hurtle into the man. After a time the girls worked out a system between them, the Furfolk child grasping one side, Siri the other.

Once, they both lost their balance and were dragged some distance before the man came around behind them and hauled them back by their tunics. Siri couldn't stop herself from giggling. The man ignored her mirth, but she noticed that the Furfolk child's face broke into a small grin, and her eyes, meeting Siri's, sparkled.

After that the man rigged lines for each of them and a pronged snowdeer antler they could use as a ground anchor. It didn't stop the sled, but at least it slowed it. The children watched silently as he showed them how to use it. Once he had taken over the lead again, they glanced at each other. When Siri grinned, the Furfolk child ducked her head to hide the smile that spread across her face.

They didn't stop for rest or food. Siri lost all sense of time until she caught sight of smoke from the Outermost Farm. They had covered in one long day the distance that had taken a day and a night with Uncle Thorvald.

By the time they reached the village, the night sun cast blue shadows from every rock and snowbank. Siri was too exhausted to feel joy, but relief spread through her at the thought that soon she would have fish soup and milk and cheese and then crawl into her bed closet. Surely once she was there, Grandmother would not let Thorvald take her away on the ship.

The activity all around the shore was strange. It looked to Siri as though almost everyone was occupied. She saw that the trade ship was back in the water. Men and women and children were carrying things, some toward the houses, some toward the smaller boats that crowded the landing.

Uncle Thorvald caught sight of them, and then it seemed that everyone else paused to note their arrival. Siri guessed that her uncle had drawn attention to it so that his scheme would begin as planned. So she wasn't surprised at having to go to the Furfolk place before she was allowed home.

Thorvald spoke with the man and then to Siri. She and the Furfolk child were to remain together under the sheltering skin boat. He and the man would bring meat to the she-bear. The villagers would watch, as they always did. The traders would probably be fascinated by the brute.

"And that's when I may go home?" Siri asked him.

"Home?" Frowning, he shook his head. "You will not go home."

"Uncle!" she cried.

"Silence!" he whispered.

"But I'm hungry," she whispered back. "I want Grandmother. If I had a mother or a sister, you would not—"

"You have a sister," he declared, his voice low, intense. "Look to her."

"What, a Furfolk child?" Siri exclaimed.

"You may be glad of her before we are done."

"When will Grandmother—"

"Hush!" he commanded. "If I hear one more word, you will be very sorry."

"Grandmother won't let you hurt me," she muttered defiantly, but only after she was sure he was out of earshot.

Before dragging the sled to the bear pit, the man cut off meat from the snowdeer haunch for each child. Siri almost declined the strip impaled on the point of his knife. But without any certainty of the fish soup she craved, she dared not risk giving up food. Only when she started eating did she realize how famished she was. Like a Furfolk child, she was careless of the bloody juice that covered her fingers and spread around her mouth.

After eating, she dozed off. Wakened suddenly, she found herself still sitting beside the Furfolk child, who was as groggy as she was. Uncle Thorvald towered over them in the sunless gloom.

"You have but a little while," he told her. "You must both be back here at first light. I will go now. Wait as long as it takes to milk two cows; then go together to the sheep. Your grandmother will be there."

Siri jumped up.

"Not yet. Do just as I have said. Most villagers are asleep or at rest, but if any see the two Furfolk children at the stable, it will seem only as before, and they will think nothing of it." He spoke a few Furfolk words to the child before he left them.

Siri peered around the edge of the skin boat. His tall figure vanished into the near darkness. How long did it take to milk two cows? Did her uncle mean cows going dry or newly freshened? What harm could there be in going too soon?

But she was afraid that he might be lurking somewhere. If he caught her disobeying, he could snatch her up without her ever seeing Grandmother.

Siri stepped away from the shelter to find some clean snow to wash with. The Furfolk girl went with her, not understanding, simply obeying the order to do whatever Siri did. Siri had to dig down to find snow clean enough for her sticky face. The rough, icy scrubbing shocked her into being fully alert. Events in the sheep stable might change the course of her uncle's plans. It all depended on Grandmother's sympathy and strength.

When Siri guessed that the time was right, she led the girl to the sheep stable. They were nearly there when Bran flew out of the darkness and hurled himself at her, knocking her down. She threw her arms around him, but he wouldn't stay still. He wiggled and licked her face and hands and flung himself on his back before her.

Then Grandmother spoke from within the stable. "Siri! Make haste!"

In the next moment Siri and Grandmother were hugging each other, with Bran circling them. The Furfolk child stood off to one side, watching.

"Grandmother, will you let me come home?" Siri mumbled, her lips against her grandmother's cheek. "I promise to be good forever."

Grandmother held her away. "First you must be good for your uncle," she said firmly. "If all goes as we hope, you both will come home. But it will take time and courage."

"But you asked him to give up this scheme. And that was even before he made me a part of it."

"Siri, much more is at stake than the fate of one or two people. I pleaded for you as I did for the Furfolk. But the decision is no longer Thorvald's alone. No one wants to make this journey, but everyone wants its outcome. So as each of us is called upon, each must strive. Now listen, my sweet minnow, for we have only a moment. Thorvald has no idea when your disguise may be thrown off, but I have finished your coat-dress, and you will find it packed away with his things. Here is cheese," she continued, pressing some into Siri's hand. "I could not bring milk because it might have been noticed. Share whatever you are given with the Furfolk child. She is without mother or brother. She is bereft."

Siri glanced over at the girl, whose face was hidden inside her hood in the dark stable.

Grandmother drew Siri to the doorway, took the sheep shears from the stone shelf, and pushed back Siri's hood. Then she took a braid, and Siri heard the blades slice through it. Shocked, Siri gasped. Her hands flew to her head.

"The hair will grow again," Grandmother murmured, but in the dim light that made the haircutting possible Siri saw tears streaking her grandmother's face.

Siri trembled when Grandmother's hand reached down her back for the other braid. The hair caught in the shears. Grandmother had to unravel the braid to finish the cutting.

"You must go now," Grandmother whispered.

"Who will see to the sheep?" Siri blurted. It wasn't what she wanted to say.

"They may go to the Outermost Farm until you return," Grandmother said. "The farmer is sending his son, Modi, on the ship, along with a few milking sheep for the journey." She pulled the hood up over Siri's head, her stiff fingers ruffling hair onto Siri's forehead to resemble the Furfolk look.

Siri clung to her. "I don't want to leave you."

"Maybe you will see trees," Grandmother told her, casting her off. "Maybe you will bring me a scented branch from the tree that never sheds its green."

"I will," Siri promised. "If ever I can," she added.

The two children returned quickly to the Furfolk place.

They were just settling down on a pile of skins when Bran bounded under the shelter. Siri knew that he should not have followed them, but she couldn't be stern with him. How could she send him home when he curled against her just as he would have done in her bed closet? After the loneliness and confusion of the last few days it felt good to lie back this way with Bran's familiar body warming her.

She was barely aware of the Furfolk child stirring nearby, turning and turning again, as if she couldn't fit in the space left empty by her brother.

13

It seemed as though she had scarcely slept when she was yanked upright and shaken awake. Uncle Thorvald pulled her out from the shelter and looked long and hard into her face. He shook his head. "Even before sunrise you are too pale." He turned aside to speak to the man, who responded by cutting meat from the snowdeer haunch.

Only it was fat, not flesh, that the man had cut. Thorvald smeared it all over Siri's face. She tried to pull away, but one large hand held the back of her head while the other rubbed the fat into her skin. All the time he did this he laid out orders. "You two children will hold the cubs while the man works with the she-bear. Understand, Siri, I cannot speak to you. You must watch the Furfolk child and do whatever she does. Remember, the bear knows her. So show no fear. The bear will smell fear. If you falter and events go against us—" He left the rest of his warning unspoken. Siri understood that he wanted her to imagine the worst.

Meanwhile the man scraped rust from a harpoon hook. Thorvald applied the rust to Siri's greased face. "You will pass for a Furfolk child only if you keep your head covered and avoid any encounters with people."

Siri shivered. "How long must I be this way?" she asked.

Thorvald shrugged. "I cannot say. Things can change in an instant. Be watchful. Be silent."

Bran gulped down the bit of fat that Thorvald dropped on the ground. Thorvald slapped his hand against his thigh and strode off in the direction of the stable, Bran at his side.

"I didn't get to say farewell," Siri protested, tears springing to her eyes. She understood that if Bran weren't shut up or tied, he could give her away. But why couldn't Uncle Thorvald allow her one moment with her faithful companion?

The man unlashed the boat shelter and hoisted it over his head. He spoke briefly to his child, who gathered up the paddle and a coil of braided walrus-hide rope. He nodded at Siri and then toward the snowdeer haunch. She picked it up. Even after meat had been cut away, it was heavy. When she began to drag it, the man said something that conveyed displeasure. So she lugged it in her arms as she staggered after him.

Thorvald was already at the bear pit, telling the few who had gathered to stand aside. He explained that the she-bear trusted only her Furfolk family. If she felt crowded or threatened, she might strike out without warning. Even he would be at risk helping to move the beasts to the ship.

The man cut a small strip from the haunch and descended into the pit. The she-bear was stuporous from the enormous feeding just hours earlier, but she took the meat in her paw and then dropped it in front of the cubs. One cub started mouthing it at once. The other yawned and watched.

The man moved slowly, the rope sliding down one arm and over the she-bear's head without tightening. He waited awhile before moving again. This time the rope was slowly pulled and quickly knotted. The man then payed out rope from the coil until he was up out of the pit. He wound the rope around a boulder before returning to the bears with another bit of meat. He did as the she-bear had done, dropping the morsel in front of the sleepy cub's nose. The cub rolled over on its back with the meat in its paws.

Still moving slowly, quietly, the man lifted first one cub and then the other. At once the one that had been chewing began to struggle and cry. Now the man moved swiftly. In the next instant Siri found herself clutching the sleepy cub, while the Furfolk child struggled to subdue the protesting one. In a kind of gurgling bark the she-bear called to her cubs.

Responding to the she-bear's alarm, even Siri's cub tried to wriggle free. The children scrambled down the rocks to the boat that Thorvald held against the shore. It rocked as they tumbled in, still gripping the frantic cubs. Paws struck out. Siri tried to keep her face away from them, but she was struck by the flailing cub the Furfolk child carried. Her cheek stung, and then she felt a trickle down her face, either tears or blood.

Scrambling from the small boat into the ship with a wild bear cub seemed hopeless. The rudder provided a kind of foothold, but it swung away from the rope ladder that hung from the deck. It was all the girls could do to hold on to the squealing and flailing cubs while pulling themselves up and into the ship.

The Furfolk child made it first and then turned to grab Siri's cub. By the time Siri was safely on board, the Furfolk child had lost her own cub. It darted back and forth in panic until it came to the low center of the ship where the animals had been kept. Unable to stop, it tumbled headlong down to that lower level, where three penned sheep were surrounded by stacks of hay and barrels of salt fish and butter and water and where an empty enclosure stood open near the mast step.

The Furfolk child dropped down, too, then reached up and took Siri's cub, which she stroked while speaking softly in Furfolk or bear language. When finally the wandering cub came over to its twin, the Furfolk child lunged and grabbed it.

Siri slid down to help. Somehow, between them, the girls managed to shove the cubs into the enclosure. But the sudden capture unleashed a fresh outpouring of cries. The she-bear's gurgling response sounded desperate but also closer.

With the gate shut, the girls were free to climb back onto the main deck. They were just in time to see the she-bear swimming alongside the skin boat. The man called to his child, who tugged Siri after her. Down they went again, this time to catch the cubs without getting themselves slashed by the tiny, sharp claws and teeth. The Furfolk child gasped as her hand was bitten, but she kept on with the task, blood oozing from punctures in her skin.

Siri held both cubs while the Furfolk child climbed up to receive them. The man said something, and the girl took the one squealing cub in her arms. Siri was trying to climb up without letting her cub escape when Thorvald spoke softly from above. "Stay there. One cub is enough." Then he was gone.

Siri heard a commotion, but no more words. Silence rushed

in behind the tumult like the pause before a great wave. The ship swung and dipped mightily. Still on the lower deck, the cub in her arms, Siri staggered and fell to her knees.

Then, terrifyingly, the she-bear loomed overhead, swaying as the ship rocked. Instinct told Siri to avert her eyes. But she couldn't pretend that she wasn't clasping the bear's cub. Siri held her breath and tried to stay absolutely still. She made herself think of quieting puppies, of calming lambs.

The man dropped down beside her. He had the cub that had lured the bear to the ship. Now he held it up, and the bear leaped down, sending forth a shower from her fur. The man went inside the enclosure. The bear followed.

"Put that cub in there," Thorvald whispered down to Siri. Glancing up, she saw that he held the neck rope. She released the cub to its mother. "Close the gate," Thorvald told her, his voice low and hoarse.

"With the man inside?" she exclaimed.

"Yes. Not a word. Not one word."

Siri shut the gate. Then Thorvald dropped the rope, and the man hauled it in. He remained there until something like calm settled over the bear and her cubs. After she had licked them and shaken off more water, she leaned back to let them nurse. She was just beginning to sniff out her new surroundings when the man rose, loosened the neck rope, and removed it.

By the time she had taken a good look at the sheep, her leg was shackled as before, the tether snaking out to an iron ring attached to a cross timber.

Siri remained at the gate while the man dipped fresh water from a barrel into a stone basin and carried it into the enclosure. The bear eyed him as he came and went. She kept her cubs tucked close. She made no move against him, nor did she shrink from him.

By this time sunlight sharpened the view of the shoreline with its low stone and turf-covered buildings. The Furfolk man rigged his boat shelter amidship just before the drop to the lower deck. He hung skins to create a kind of barrier for the children, then stacked his own trade goods at one end—the walrus tusks and a perfect spiraling narwhal tooth—all carefully packed beneath furs.

More cargo was carried aboard. While it was stowed below the deck and people crowded the ship, Siri stayed inside the skin shelter. She wondered if Thorvald or the man had noticed the Furfolk child's bleeding hand or her own scratched cheek, now grown stiff and tight and hot. But no attention was paid them except, indirectly, with Thorvald's reminder to everyone commencing the journey to keep away from the wild animals and the wild people.

14

As soon as the rowers took up their oars, Siri pulled aside the skin flap that served as a door to the shelter. Peeping out, she saw what looked like every last person in Starkland ranged along the shore. They were waving off the ship with its combined crew of seafaring traders and hunters and farmers and its precious cargo, the ice bears. Siri looked in vain for Grandmother and then for Bran. When she caught sight of Gudrun, Siri nearly gave herself away by waving and shouting to her.

She wondered how long it would take before her absence was noted. What would Grandmother tell the Elders? Would they be angry because they had been tricked or grateful because Thorvald had found a way to hold the Furfolk man? Probably if the bear and her cubs were safely delivered and the banishment ended, Thorvald would return to Starkland a hero. Maybe Siri would be something of a hero, too. After all, she in her disguise was helping to make this journey possible.

The ship, propelled by ten oarsmen, moved swiftly down the fjord. But when they had to maneuver around ice floes, they got in one another's way. There were harsh exchanges between seafarers skilled in working together and the crew from the settlement. Even those who were fishermen were unaccustomed to so large a ship and rowing with so many others.

Grim, the leader of the traders, was helmsman. He and Thorvald conferred quietly. Grim seemed concerned about the inexperienced Starkland men, especially since one was only a lad.

Thorvald replied that the lad, Modi, might yet be one of the best of the lot. Then Thorvald spoke up to quell disputes among those on the rowing benches. After that, Grim addressed all the oarsmen. If the rowers put aside their differences and pulled together, they would make enough headway to be at sea by midday and able to hoist the sail. He expected good, strong westerlies to drive them south by east the rest of the way.

The oarsmen stopped grumbling and blaming one another and bent to their task. The ship seemed to skim over the water until the ocean swell made its way into the mouth of the fjord. Now the ship climbed and plunged. This was nothing like riding out a squall in a small fishing boat in the fjord. The rowers grunted as they struggled toward each summit, then quickened their oar strokes, sometimes at cross-purposes, while sheets of icy water slashed across the deck.

Clinging to the lashing, the Furfolk child held her injured hand out to be washed. She sucked in her breath, perhaps because of the cold or else the salt, but she continued to expose her hand to this painful treatment, while Siri cowered from the onslaught and shivered helplessly.

She wasn't cold, though. What sent her crouching in misery at the rear of the shelter was the picture in her mind of the white falcon she had once spotted stuck to an iceberg in the fjord. The falcon must have blundered into the misted mound and been stunned. Perhaps the surface ice had melted and then frozen again. The falcon had flailed its magnificent wings, desperate to break free. As Siri watched in horror, the current had slowly spun the iceberg until it rocked and pitched over.

Siri had turned from the upheaval, the awful splash. When she looked again, the berg was newly shaped, its exposed underside a striking blue. That lovely floating mountain of ice, partly submerged, was something like this ship. If a big sea slapped it onto its side and rolled it over, Siri knew she would be trapped underneath like the falcon.

Just the thought of it was sickening. She crouched on her skin sleeping mat, her face turned from the waste bucket, and longed for the motion to stop. It wasn't until the sail was hoisted and the oars shipped that she managed to crawl to the opening and watch the men with sail ropes setting the ship on its course.

Grim assigned each newcomer to an experienced seafarer to gain knowledge of the sail. Thorvald, who set himself to learn the ways of the rudder, divided the crew so that each watch had its share of able seafarers. But only Grim could read the sun and stars, the currents and winds. The lives of everyone on board and the future of the banished settlers depended on his navigation.

The square sail, held at an angle, took possession of the ship. Siri could feel the timbers tremble and obey. She began to lean and balance as the ship surged forward.

When one seafarer doled out milk and salt fish and cheese

to the others, Modi took a portion to the Furfolk. Ducking her head to hide her face, Siri carried the food into the shelter.

She was gulping down the rich, comforting milk when she heard someone say that Furfolk had no use for any food but fish and meat. Quickly Siri pressed the remaining milk on the girl, who paused only briefly before tasting and then gulping it down. Siri nudged the girl with the empty mug, forcing her out where she would be clearly visible with the streak of white froth fresh above her lips. Siri, her face hidden behind the girl, made her stand there until Modi took back the empty mug and pointed to the child's lips with traces of milk still showing.

As soon as it was established that the Furfolk might after all take what food was stowed on board, some of the men expressed relief because it meant that most of the meat could go to the she-bear, keeping her content and perhaps amiable.

Siri was relieved, too. Just knowing that milk and cheese were forthcoming lifted her spirits. Then it occurred to her that if she could teach the Furfolk girl to consume milk and cheese, she might also teach her how to speak like a person. By now Siri was certain that this was the child who was already a natural mimic.

"Cheese," Siri whispered as she nibbled some and then broke off a bit for the Furfolk child.

"Cheese," echoed the girl. She put it in her mouth, then made a face.

"Good," said Siri, remembering to keep her voice low. She took another bite. "Good cheese."

The girl ate some more.

"Good?" asked Siri, nodding her head.

"Good," answered the child.

When Siri offered cheese to the Furfolk man, he brushed it aside. Never mind, she thought. He could take care of himself, or else Thorvald would have to feed him. She shared the rest of the cheese with the girl and then sank down in a daze of exhaustion.

It was good to hear footsteps on the deck and voices coming and going. Perhaps the journey would not be so terrible after all. Forced to this disguise, she had already found one way around it. In time she would think of other small ways to prevail against this confinement her uncle had imposed on her.

15

By the fifth morning Siri realized she was losing all sense of time. If she was uncertain of how long they had been under way, if she had to think back to yesterday and the day before to recollect the small same events that barely set each similar day apart, there was a chance that this voyage might swallow her up altogether. Suddenly it seemed necessary to keep track, to mark the passing of each day.

She found a splinter of bone the man had used to draw pictures on a bear tooth. The man had discarded the splinter when the tip broke off, but it was sharp enough for Siri to scratch a yellow groove in the skin boat that roofed their shelter. She made five strokes for five days and then hid the splinter under her sleeping mat.

She wanted to ask Uncle Thorvald how far they had come and how much longer the journey would take. But even when he came to talk with the man in Furfolk speech, he avoided all contact with her. He wouldn't even meet her eyes.

The sameness of the ocean was oppressive. The evening the Furfolk man harpooned a porpoise from the deck and was able to haul it into the ship, the Starkland men rejoiced. Not that they were hungry, but they were starved for any action. The sight of a distant whale drew the most comment from them. It showed up the difference between the mariners, who were used to being at sea, and the men from the settlement, who chafed at the vastness all around them.

Thorvald gave them small tasks to perform to make them feel occupied. But when he and the Furfolk man bound the she-bear so that the enclosure could be cleaned, no one would go close enough to the savage beast to risk a swipe of her powerful forepaw. With Thorvald and the man across from each other holding the bear, the children had to be called in.

Thorvald remarked loudly that as the she-bear was used to the Furfolk, the young ones would be safe. Siri supposed it was his way of informing her of what she was expected to do. So when the man spoke to the Furfolk child, Siri followed her into the enclosure.

It was impossible to shovel bear droppings into the manure basket with the cubs so curious and wild. To clean the enclosure, the girls had to let the cubs scamper around the lower deck. As long as the she-bear could see them chasing each other in circles and tumbling in mock battle, she didn't strain against the ropes that could choke her. But when it was time to herd the cubs back inside and they resisted and then became alarmed, the she-bear began to struggle and cough.

The man spoke to Thorvald. They each payed out rope, allowing the bear to drop to all fours and move toward the gate. Siri kept one eye on the ropes while she stalked the cubs. Was the bear so intent on her babies that she would fail to notice that Siri wasn't one of the Furfolk?

The bear uttered a deep-throated rumble that ended in a snuffle. Instantly the cubs turned to scramble back to her. The girls were right behind them to shut the gate.

While Thorvald and the man eased the she-bear out of the ropes and cut down a quarter of the reeking carcass for her, the crew not handling the sail stood around to watch.

Siri seized the moment. She had been longing to get close to the sheep. Now she dragged the laden basket to the sheep pen, where she began to pick out soiled bedding to add to the bear droppings. Glancing up, she saw that the men were still watching the bears. Quickly she grabbed the Furfolk child's sleeve and tugged her down beside a sheep.

Pressing against the woolly flank and reaching underneath, Siri squirted a stream of milk at the Furfolk child. It took only a moment for the girl to understand. Kneeling, she opened her mouth. When Siri's aim went wrong and the milk splashed the girl's face, she began to laugh. Hastily Siri milked some into her own mouth. But she worried that the laughter would draw attention to them. She had to give up and whisk the reluctant Furfolk child back to the shelter.

Only then did Siri think of the manure basket that needed to be emptied. Her first thought was that her uncle would be cross about it. But when he simply lifted it onto the upper deck himself and dumped its contents over the side, it came to her that since she was supposed to be a Furfolk child, he couldn't appear to be angry with her.

That was something to keep in mind during the endless procession of days and nights to come. It seemed that Siri's disguise removed her somewhat from her uncle's absolute control.

"Milk," she told the Furfolk child, wiping it from her face.

"Good," declared the girl, still chortling.

"Yes, good!" Siri exclaimed. Then, her voice dropping, she

pointed to the bear tearing at the meat and said, "Bear. Ice bear."

"Ice bear," the child said back to her. "Good."

"Milk is good," Siri declared.

The girl looked puzzled. She didn't speak again.

Siri had to make herself slow down, to simplify each lesson, one word at a time. Her own eagerness made her impatient. She imagined a time when she and a girl might have a real conversation. Siri would tell her about things unknown in her world, like trees.

It took many more attempts before Siri was able to make the girl understand that *good* was not the word for *milk* and could be applied as well to cheese.

"Fingers," Siri told the child, showing her. "Hair," she said, touching her own and then the other's.

The girl lapsed into silence again, defeated by too much at once. But later, when the man gave her a bit of slimy meat that made Siri turn away with revulsion, the Furfolk girl pursued Siri, tapping on her shoulder to get her attention. "Ice bear," she declared in triumph, flourishing the stinking slab of flesh.

Siri couldn't help herself. "Meat," she said, correcting the child. She pointed. "Ice bear."

The child tilted her head to one side. She seemed to consider these meanings. "Meat?" she asked, examining what she was about to put in her mouth.

Siri nodded.

Suddenly the girl's face lit up. "Milk good. Cheese good. Meat good."

"Yes!" cried Siri. She clapped her hand over her mouth to stifle the shout.

The girl pulled Siri's hand aside and pushed the meat against her lips.

Siri could feel her stomach clench, but she took a bite, anyway. She had to.

The child fed herself and Siri until the meat was gone. As soon as the girl went outside to look at seabirds overhead, Siri was sick into their waste bucket. Afterward she felt spent and ill. Still, something more than words had been exhanged between them. Even with her stomach heaving, she had no regrets.

16

The mariners claimed seabirds meant that land was near. But Grim said this could not be so unless they were far off course. Maybe an ocean current had set them to the east, but they should not assume this at once. Even with the polestar faint in the night sky, he judged that they were still heading for Thyrne. Of course, he warned, the return voyage to Starkland would be a different matter. Not only would they be fighting adverse winds, but later in the summer the polestar tended to vanish in the northern sky.

The night brought thick fog and baffling crosswinds. By morning Grim had called for the oars to be fitted into their holes, rowers ready on their benches. There they waited while other men played the sail to catch the shifting winds. The fog prevented those in the rear from seeing others up forward. Even the top of the sail vanished from sight. Except for Grim's occasional commands, all talk was suspended.

Everything dripped, and every surface was slippery and treacherous. When the wind dropped entirely, Grim ordered the men to pull in their oars. Until he could be more certain of their position, he preferred to let the ship wallow at the mercy of the ocean currents than to drive it mistakenly toward some unknown landfall.

All the following day the ship rolled and righted itself in aimless, fretful motion. The limp sail snapped from time to time as if it had caught the beginning of wind, but whenever the men hauled in or let out lines to take advantage of what might be a freshening breeze, it came to nothing.

Then, during the second night becalmed, the dripping fog turned to rain. Daybreak came with only the hint of light. The rain fell harder, the wind finally rising and then veering until it blew from the northeast. When Grim called for the sail to be reefed, two of his men objected. They needed all the sail to keep a forward momentum. Grim predicted that very soon they would have more wind than they could manage. It was best to be prepared.

Siri listened and watched from beneath the overhanging skin boat. The men seemed still in thrall to yesterday's windless fog. Slow and dull, they bent under the rain and turned from the wind. That meant they also turned from Grim at the helm. What she couldn't tell was which of them were real seafarers and which the crew from Starkland. All backs seemed to deflect orders in the same way they resisted the elements.

Thorvald ducked inside the shelter to speak with the man. Siri saw that her uncle was drenched, his garments sagging with water. For the first time since the day they departed, he spoke directly to Siri. He told her what he had said to the man, that Grim believed they were about to be hit by a big storm. If they began to ship water while all the men were occupied on deck, she and the Furfolk should bail out the lower deck. And they might have to tie down the sheep.

"And the bears?" asked Siri.

"The man will see to the she-bear. You and the girl may have to ride out the storm with the cubs."

"Where?" asked Siri, afraid he meant they must stay in the enclosure. But Thorvald didn't stay to reply. He was making his way past the mast to lash down barrels that were beginning to shift and teeter beside the sheep pen.

Siri started to follow him, but the rain drove her back under cover.

"Man," said the girl, pointing after Thorvald. "Father."

Siri, who had taught her that *father* was the word for the Furfolk man, understood that the girl was applying what she had learned to Thorvald. "Uncle," Siri tried to explain. "My uncle. Man. Siri's Uncle Thorvald." She pointed to the Furfolk man. "Man. Girl's father." It was so hard without names for either of them.

This time, although confused, the girl seemed to be wrestling with these meanings. She pointed to the she-bear, then to the cubs, who were frolicking in the downpour. "Bear," she asked, "father?" She held an imaginary baby to her.

Siri told her the bear was a mother, the cubs baby bears.

"Baby," said the girl. "Mother."

Siri nodded. "Your mother has a baby."

The girl's face lit up. "Mother baby?"

"You will go home to mother and baby. You . . . girl . . . sister . . . will go home to boy . . . brother. Siri will go home to grandmother."

But that was too much to try to absorb all at once. Besides, the girls needed to secure belongings in the shelter. Siri tried to empty the bucket before tying it down. She shoved it and was crawling and nudging it forward when the boat lurched and thrust her down to the lower deck. One of the men caught the bucket as it rolled across the deck, spilling its contents, while Siri pulled herself upright.

Before climbing up to the shelter, she made her way past the bears to the sheep. The butter tub had broken loose and crashed into the pen, where it rolled back and forth with the pitching of the boat. One sheep had fallen. The other two trampled it to escape the constant attack of the heavy tub. Siri was able to roll it out of the way, but it left a jagged break in the side of the pen. Looking for rope, Siri could barely keep her eyes open against the lashing wind and rain. Finally she dragged the injured sheep over to block the gap. It was all she could do before getting herself back to the shelter.

The man was not under the skin boat. Maybe he had gone out to help Thorvald. The girl clutched at Siri, holding on so hard that Siri could barely move to the rear to fasten down the bucket. Once her hands were free, she drew the girl against her and said, "Now I will tell you a story." This was what Grandmother had done with her for as long as Siri could remember. "I will tell you a story about two ravens named Thought and Memory."

"Named?" said the girl, scowling at another meaning for this word. "Siri?"

"No." Siri tried to explain. "I mean, yes, Siri is a name, but so is Thorvald." Only how could the girl grasp the idea of naming when Furfolk held names secret? "Two ravens," Siri continued, giving up on the explanation. She held out two fingers. "Two. Thought and Memory are their names, and this is their story."

But the storm blew so hard that when Siri opened her

mouth to speak, the wind tore into her face, contorting her lips and locking her frozen mouth. It blew like this all the day. Then either the ship swung or the fierce wind changed direction.

Siri rubbed her icy skin. She rubbed and rubbed. Then, slurring her words because her mouth was so stiff, she started all over again. "I will tell you a story about the First Ravens."

The Furfolk child huddled next to Siri and gazed into her face as if she could follow every word.

"The Frost Giant still rules Starkland. Where he rules, no tree may grow. But across the sea in the land of Thyrne a First Tree grew strong and tall. It was the father and the mother of all trees."

"Mother?" asked the Furfolk child.

"That's right. Mother and father. And on it lived two ravens, the First Ravens, mother and father of all ravens."

"Ravens?"

Siri wanted to continue her story, even though she wasn't at all sure that she knew what came next. Grandmother's stories were like the strands she wove, looping in and out to make her homespun cloth. "After the storm," Siri told the girl, "I will explain about ravens and trees. Now is the time for the story."

Just then the man lurched in, carrying the bear cubs. Each girl took one from him and scrambled back as far as she could, bracing against each other to keep from sliding as they held their wriggling burdens.

Siri caught a glimpse of the man as he jumped or fell to the lower deck to reach the she-bear. As the Furfolk child quieted her cub with murmurs and stroking and rocking, Siri tried to mimic her. Risking the snapping jaws, Siri cuddled the one she held and spoke into its fur. "Where the Frost Giant rules," she told it, "no tree may grow—"

The cub found a way to nestle with its chin across Siri's arm, its nose just touching the cub in the Furfolk child's arms. Worn out from their long, wild storm play, both cubs went limp.

"Where the Frost Giant rules . . ." Siri began again. But the story was no longer needed. Although powerful wind gusts still slammed the ship, the full force of the storm was abating.

Soon it was possible for men to run along the deck. The girls could hear their feet pounding as they chased whatever had broken loose. The Furfolk man, who had ridden out the storm with the she-bear, bailed water from the enclosure and the rest of the lower deck before replacing the cubs.

The injured sheep was killed. After dry willow twigs were found in a leathern sack, enough to make a fire in a soapstone basin, the men still had to wait one more full day before the sea grew calm enough for them to cook the meat. By that time the cubs were tugging and snarling over a scrap of the woolly pelt, and the she-bear was pacing and eyeing the carcass lashed to the mast step.

When the meat began to sizzle on the deck behind the shelter, Siri felt like pacing, too. Once it was cooked, it didn't take long for the twelve men to consume most of the sheep. Thorvald saw to it that the bones, with some meat left on them, were given to the Furfolk, who fell upon them. While the girls stripped every bit of gristle they could find, the man broke the marrow bones for them and for himself.

The she-bear got what was left. Siri could hear her crunch bone and horn and hooves, devouring everything. Nothing remained but the scrap of woolen skin, the cubs' plaything, and it didn't take them long to tear that to shreds.

17

Even reefed, the sail had torn from stitching that bound it to the top of the cross pole. Grim made the men drop the mast to look for damage that might cause trouble in the next storm.

It took more than a day to set this and other mishaps to rights. But some things were beyond repair. The cover had blown off one of the water kegs. It had spilled half its contents before it was covered again, and by then the seas breaking over the ship had tainted the water. This caused great concern until it was found that the trader's small boat had filled with rain to a depth of three hands. So the bear was given the brackish water, the keg was rinsed, and the rainwater was transferred, dipper by dipper, from the boat to the keg.

Beginning to dry out, Siri stretched her arms toward the sun-filled sky. But her leggings and hooded coat stiffened on her, and she dreamed of washing from head to toe.

During the lull the Furfolk man told Thorvald to lower him in his skin boat to fish. Thorvald consulted Grim, who shook his head. They wanted less commotion on board just now, not more. With the sail mended and the mast stepped, the ship would soon be surging ahead. Grim said the Furfolk man could trawl a line as long as he kept out of the way of the sailing crew.

When the man carried his line and hooks and harpoon to the rear of the ship, Siri was quick to take advantage of his absence. First she dipped the waste bucket over the side until it was thoroughly rinsed. Next, keeping her voice low so that no one but the Furfolk child could hear her, she declared that they were going to borrow water from the bears. She jumped down to the lower deck with the wooden bucket and beckoned to the girl.

The girl looked doubtful about entering the enclosure without orders, without her father to supervise.

Siri had no way of knowing whether it was the she-bear's wrath or the man's that gave the child pause. To convince her, Siri had to forge ahead with all the confidence she could muster. Anyway, even if most of her whispered words meant nothing to the girl, they gave Siri enough courage to propel her into the enclosure, and that brought the Furfolk child as far as the gate.

The cubs helped. They flung themselves at the girls, one of them shaking the bit of wooled skin like a puppy challenging another to play. Siri glanced upward to make sure that no one noticed and wondered aloud why the Furfolk children were with the bears. Then she glanced at the she-bear. Since she could reach the deep stone basin that contained water for her, she could as easily lunge at Siri.

The she-bear rose, stretched, and eyed her cubs as they clambered over each other to gain the girls' attention. "You play with them," Siri instructed. Stooping down to caress a cub, she rolled it on its back to show the nervous Furfolk child. "Now," she commanded. "Hurry."

The girl crouched, one hand on the unlatched gate for a quick retreat, the other reaching out to the cubs.

Glancing again at the bear, Siri scooped water from the basin into the bucket. If only she had a dipper or a mug. If only her hands were bigger. She couldn't help wasting some water as she cupped her hands and swept it over the stone rim and down into the wooden bucket. While she sloshed the water, she murmured nonsense to the cubs in a storytelling voice until first one cub was drawn to her and then the other. Soon they were darting at the splashes, their infant paws playfully practicing lunges that could one day kill a seal or a person.

"Siri!" hissed the Furfolk child. "Siri!"

Siri skidded around to find herself face-to-face with the she-bear. For one instant she was voiceless. Then she resumed her singsong recital of events to come. "And you will have fresh fish," she crooned, deliberately splashing the ecstatic cubs. They chased the droplets that sprayed from her hands. "And as the storm already washed you," she continued, addressing the she-bear without looking at her, "you will lend me some of your water." She could smell the bear's hot breath.

Dragging the bucket with her, she backed toward the gate. The cubs started to follow. She had to dip into her precious water supply to spray them again, to distract them. The she-bear swung her head in Siri's direction. Somehow Siri understood that this signaled recognition. Still, she kept on backing until she felt sure she must be out of striking range. Then she offered up a parting handful of water.

The she-bear's jaws snapped as drops cascaded over the black nose and white fur above. Then, head bowed, the bear wiped a huge forepaw across her face and all the way down to her tapering muzzle. After that she slid onto her side and batted cublike at imaginary spray.

With a stab of pity, Siri felt the toll this long confinement must be taking on the captive animal.

"She needs to swim," Siri whispered as soon as the gate was fastened. "She needs to hunt."

Siri lugged the bucket and gestured to the Furfolk child to climb ahead of her to keep it from tipping when she hoisted it up to the deck. When they were under cover, she told the girl to take off all her garments, demonstrating with her own. This went smoothly until Siri began to scrub herself, using her stockings as washcloths. The girl let out a stream of Furfolk words. Siri overrode them with words of her own. "We will be clean. You'll see, girl. Sister. You'll like it."

But when she ducked her entire head in the bucket, sloshing water through her hair, the Furfolk child seized her shoulders and yanked her up. Spluttering, Siri wrenched herself free and dipped her head once more.

By the time she was finished and had wrung out her hair, the naked child was dancing furiously on bare feet and in Furfolk language declaring Siri's stunt an outrage. Siri was shivering violently. She was ready to move the project on. So she simply grabbed the girl and dunked her headfirst. It was hard to keep her down, though. The smaller child was lithe and strong as an ice bear cub. Within seconds she had wriggled free, gasping forth her indignation.

Siri was glad she had taken the child by surprise. She wouldn't get a second chance to overpower her. But she managed to grab the girl's undershirt and thrust it with Siri's shift and stockings into the bucket. The girl tried to rescue her garment, but Siri kept all the clothing immersed while she plunged everything up and down and scrubbed for all she was worth.

After that, Siri was at a loss. Her skin was turning blue. The Furfolk child clutched herself. They needed sun, but Siri feared being discovered like this. All she had that was dry was Grandmother's long-tailed cap, which couldn't make enough difference. So Siri unrolled a snowdeer hide and a frost-fox skin for warming. She knew she would be in terrible trouble if the man found that she had gone into his fur pack, but it was all she could think of. She tied the washed things in the wind before huddling with the girl.

The Furfolk child's heavier tunic took longer to dry. As soon as Siri was dressed, the woven cap again hidden inside her boot, she raked her fingers through her hair for want of a comb and then shook out the girl's skin shirt and held it up to the wind. She longed to shove back her grimy hood, to let her hair blow free. But she had no idea when Thorvald might suddenly appear, so she kept her head covered until she was back in the shelter.

She told the Furfolk child that she would feel better now that she was clean. "Clean," Siri emphasized, indicating the bucket with its now-soiled water. "Washed. Clean." She pointed to herself. "Siri clean. Siri's clothes clean. Siri's hair clean," she finished, shaking her head and tossing her hair.

The girl chortled. "Clean," she echoed, shaking her own head of shiny black hair. "Sister clean."

"Yes," Siri replied as she tucked away the frost-fox fur and the snowdeer hide. "Sister clean, beautiful."

The Furfolk child peered into the bucket and raised one hand as if to probe the wash water.

Siri stopped her. "No. Dirty now."

At this rebuff the dark eyes clouded.

"Sister clean," Siri told her. Then, because she didn't know how to sort through this confusion, she drew the child outside the shelter. Sitting very close and speaking in an undertone, Siri promised a long-ago story about a wonderful maiden named Lif, who was clean and strong and survived the most terrible storm of all time.

The Furfolk child shoved aside the shiny hair that blew across her eyes and raised her face to the sun. "Story," she said. "Siri story."

And then a basket of fish was dumped before them, and they were set to work feeding the she-bear and preparing for more cooking.

18

For the next four days a stiff breeze drove the ship straight toward the north coast of Thyrne. Then the air softened. It felt like a warm, moist breath hovering over the water. Seafowl came and vanished in the gray sky. Then, out of nowhere, a vessel with the trim lines of a warship appeared on the eastern horizon. It swung about and headed for the trade ship.

Excitement on board ranged from eagerness to apprehension. It wouldn't take long for the smaller craft to overtake the broader, heavier vessel. But soon the traders recognized the steeply raked prow that curved into an elegant scroll. The oncoming boat belonged to the king's fleet.

Grim ordered the sailing men to let out lines. The sail flapped, and the trade ship slowed. Giving Thorvald the helm, Grim leaped across the deck to stand upon a rowing bench. Spreading his legs to balance as the ship wallowed, he greeted the helmsman on the smaller vessel.

"Grim!" declared that man. "I did not think I would see you again this year. I thought you intended to sail west of Starkland."

"I do," Grim replied. "But some who agreed to come with me were unprepared when I set out for Starkland. I hope they will join me now. And it is just as well they did not sail on this last voyage, for we bring an ice bear and her cubs for the king."

"An ice bear!" exclaimed the helmsman, turning to inform his crew. "Still alive?"

"Yes, a Furfolk man keeps them. And there are six men from Starkland who hope they may deliver the beasts to the underking or his henchmen."

"Better than that," said the other helmsman, "the king himself. He is here in the northern realm, although not for long. I can sail ahead to bring word that you come."

"We can make haste," Grim replied. "Save for one spell without wind, the journey has been swift. For the sake of the bears, we have kept a careful course."

"Then do not abandon care now. I can sail directly from here. This vessel skims across water too hazardous for your laden trade ship, which is broad of beam and deeply keeled. You dare not risk the currents and shoals around the islands north of the mainland. You know well that your safest approach adds perhaps two days. Besides, the king's people will need time to ready a stronghold for the bear."

When the smaller ship took off, Grim explained to Thorvald that they must head seaward awhile before their final approach to the coast.

Two more days! "Two," Siri declared, holding up fingers for the Furfolk child to count. "Two days, two nights."

The language lessons had advanced so rapidly that gestures like this were seldom needed. By the time they reached home the girl ought to have at least as good a command of this language as Thorvald had of Furfolk. The lessons would be much easier after Thorvald revealed Siri's identity and they could practice speaking together openly. When would that be? Siri couldn't imagine what Thorvald was waiting for. Surely she wouldn't be forced to suffer the return journey still in disguise.

She looked around their shelter. At least it provided protection from high seas and rain. It was far better than weathering a storm on the open deck with only a rowing bench to cling to.

"After Uncle Thorvald allows me to be Siri again," she said to the child, "I will still stay with you. We will eat and wash and sleep just as we have done. I will tell you stories, and you will speak to me more and more and more."

The Furfolk child scowled. "What means moreandmore-andmoreand?"

Siri burst out laughing. After a brief pause the Furfolk child laughed with her. "Moreandmoreandmoreand," she repeated, and they rolled about with mirth.

The Furfolk man poked his head inside the shelter and growled a few words. The girls stopped at once, eyes cast down to avoid his condemning stare. But as soon as they heard him jump to the lower deck, their eyes met, and they had to clap their hands over their mouths to stifle more giggles.

Siri found herself wondering why she had made no attempt to learn the Furfolk language. On the return voyage they should change places, the Furfolk child becoming the teacher. Then it would be Siri's turn to struggle over strange sounds with their meanings buried inside them. The Furfolk child had made it clear that trying to grasp Siri's words was like seeking a way in the endless night of winter. When understanding dawned, it gave shape to language much the way the first glimmer of sun restored a sense of place to the featureless dark.

The two days passed without sight of land. People grew edgy. Tempers flared. Siri heard Grim and Thorvald consulting with the Furfolk man. Grim thought the sheep should be killed before they grew any thinner. Since the storm had ruined most of their fodder, their milk had dwindled almost to nothing.

Thorvald translated for the Furfolk man, who doubted the starving sheep could provide meat enough for the she-bear, let alone for hungry men. Here were seals for the taking. The rocky islets held weed for the sheep and seal for all who craved meat.

Before the skin boat was lowered into the water, the Furfolk man spoke to the girl. Then he and Thorvald, with paddles, lines, and harpoon between them, pushed off from the ship.

"Sister go to bears," the girl declared as the two girls sat with their legs dangling over the lower deck.

With the protection of the boat shelter gone, Siri glanced about before speaking. Even with the sail slapping noisily, someone might overhear them talking.

"No," Siri objected, her voice low. "She-bear hungry. Sister's father and Uncle Thorvald bring seal. After bear belly full, Sister go to bear."

"Father say," the child insisted.

"Look!" Siri whispered, directing the child's gaze toward black ledges rimmed with white foam. Seals rested on every surface, some partly submerged, others splashed by breaking waves. The skin boat passed heads poking out of the water, all seal eyes fixed on the ship. The skin boat didn't seem to alarm them.

Thorvald paddled, nudging the boat close to the ledge. The man hurled the harpoon, then pulled back to offset Thorvald's weight as he bent to the seal. Siri saw his knife flash. By then the Furfolk man had struck another seal, again leaving it for Thorvald to kill and lash to the boat while he struck once more.

Now the seals scrambled and rolled and slid into the breaking sea. The men in the skin boat tore rockweed and cut rubbery kelp to bring back to the ship. Around them gulls and fulmers and skuas screeched and keened, attacking the bloody carcasses the boat hauled in the water.

The she-bear paced, rose onto her hindquarters, swung around, and then paced on all fours again. Her cubs clamored to keep up, to nuzzle her, but she thrust them off. They sensed her frenzy just as she sensed from the birds and the scent of blood that seals were near.

It took a moment before Siri realized that something was wrong. Then she caught her breath. The she-bear wasn't tethered.

Had the line attached to her hind leg come free? No. Siri saw it had been unfastened. The Furfolk man must have released her before taking off in the skin boat. But why? And why had he told his child to stay with the bear?

Much later, after the bear had rolled onto her back to sleep off the seal she had consumed, Siri pondered this some more. The bear was fettered again, the line from her hind leg securely tied to the crosspiece. Siri gazed at the enclosure, at the cubs idly pawing seal parts strewn about. Long after the skin boat had become a cover again, after the sheep had been fed fresh kelp and the ship's crew had feasted on seal meat, Siri kept on wondering.

Watching the Furfolk man and girl gorging on raw flesh turned Siri's stomach. It made even cooked meat unappealing. So she helped herself to a small portion of cheese and some kelp, which she chewed and chewed while she puzzled over the bear and the girl and the man.

No one had noticed that during the seal hunt every person remaining on board had been at risk. Think of the harm the bear could have inflicted if she had been roused, if she had discovered that she could break out of the enclosure.

Yet nothing had happened. Nothing happened because she was not aroused.

So what would have aroused her? Siri asked herself. A threat to her cubs? The man shouting an alarm? Why had he placed his own child at risk?

The day Siri had boldly entered the enclosure for water, the Furfolk child's reluctance to join her had seemed like fear. At the time Siri had assumed the child feared for herself. But the Furfolk child must have known that no harm would come to her. Still, she would have been less certain how the bear would react to Siri.

Siri was beginning to make sense of this. The man had untied the rope before leaving the ship. He had deliberately let the bear loose because he could count on her in his absence. He knew she would rise up if anything or anyone threatened his child, just as she would protect her cubs. So the Furfolk man, who seemed so agreeable, was more wary than he appeared. Probably he trusted no one except Thorvald.

Understanding had come to Siri through a shift in her viewpoint. While it allowed her to sort out questions that resisted the usual answers, it was unsettling. She had to cast off assumptions of a lifetime. This was like a new telling of an old story, and it set her apart from her own people and closer to the Furfolk.

It made her wonder. Who was the teller of this story? Where would it end?

19

The men of Starkland gazed in wonderment at their first sight of land. Bare cliffs reared up from the sea. Birds, shrilling and wailing, filled all the crevices and roosted on every jutting edge, and the sky seethed with them on the wing. But beyond the sea cliffs, everywhere along the coastline, the hills were green.

Siri longed to question the traders about Thyrne. Where were the walls and the roads Grandmother had described? Where were farms and towns, cows and wagons, and all the wonders of the kingdom that had banished entire families to Starkland before it had a name, when it was known only as the Land of the White Falcons? Where were trees?

She stared so hard she stopped seeing anything. Then she crawled to the dark corner of the shelter and slept.

She awoke to a kind of half-light that distorted everything onshore. A dark, turf-covered mound seemed to be a dwelling, but it was larger than any building she had seen and therefore must be a hillock. Was it near or far? Siri couldn't tell. But it was ringed by a ditch. Or was that some kind of circular river? Siri peered with all her might. But already it was receding as the ship moved on.

She stood inside the flap of the shelter to keep out of the

rain that was just beginning to fall. She hoped it would pour so hard that it would wash away the greasy mess on the floor of the bear enclosure. Maybe when they arrived, her uncle would let her cast off the Furfolk skin garments and dress in her own clothes. She would scrub herself before she put them on. She would wash away the stench of this journey, the accumulated filth of bear droppings and seal fat and slimy snowdeer hide.

The Furfolk child stirred, groaned, and sat up. "Siri?" she said.

"Come and look," Siri invited, wondering whether Grandmother had provided clothes enough for two girls. Surely the Furfolk child would want what Siri looked forward to.

Together they gazed through steady rain at small houses of stone and wood, at stacks of brown sod, at fences, and at yards with animals. One of the sheep on the lower deck began to blat. Sheep on land answered, their calls muffled and then fading as the ship slid past.

The rain droned on. Grim called for the oars. Suddenly the ship was astir. The men rushed to their tasks, sliding into one another on the slippery deck, careless now that they were coming into a safe harbor. Somehow, without mishap, the sail was dropped and rolled, the mast unstepped. There were too many rowers. Every man claimed his turn, his watch.

The bear raised her muzzle landward, sniffing, while her cubs splashed and skidded around the enclosure.

The Furfolk man came out to see what all the commotion was about. With his hand shielding his eyes from the rain, he noted the boats pulled up on the shore, the smoke rising from buildings, the emerging colors that, moment by moment, became more visible. Even under the steady rain it was clear now that light was increasing. It must be very early in the morning.

Siri dashed inside the shelter, found her bone splinter, and scored another notch. This was the seventeenth day. What a long time it seemed. Yet, with an adverse wind, the return voyage would take even longer. Her heart sank at the thought of so much time at sea. Then she brushed discouragement aside. First she would see Thyrne. There would be more strangers than ever had landed in Starkland, especially women and children. She would note their clothing and manner, their talk and their food. She would make pictures in her mind so that every detail would come clear for Grandmother.

Yes, and she would look for trees.

After they had anchored, all the traders but Grim went ashore to locate a booth for the goods they had brought. The Starkland men were eager to set foot on solid ground, too, but Grim advised them to wait until the king or the underking came to receive them.

Since the warm rain would hasten the rotting of the remaining seal meat, Thorvald suggested feeding it to the bear. But the man said she was not yet hungry. So the seal hung off the ship, attracting harbor fish that could be netted, and the men entertained themselves catching some and tossing them to the cubs.

The Furfolk man scowled at this and withdrew inside the shelter. When Siri went in to use the waste bucket, she saw that he was bent over the bear tooth, blowing dust raised by his sharpstone and rubbing the ivory with his thumb.

Glad to be out of the rain, Siri stayed in her dark corner

until the girl scuttled in. Speaking in a rush to the man, she turned to Siri, tugging off the hood in her attempt to drag Siri outside.

"Man. So. Men. Man," the Furfolk child exclaimed.

Siri didn't share this excitement. Still, if the traders returning to the ship had brought something interesting, Siri supposed she ought to be on hand when they brought it aboard.

All the Starkland men were crowded together with Grim to greet the men as their boat slid alongside the ship. Siri seized the moment to let the rain wash over her head. It felt so good she rubbed and rubbed at her hair. She was about to suggest to the girl that she do the same when the Starkland crew and Grim fell back before the boarding men.

They were not the traders. That was why the girl had been so excited that she could only offer a jumble of men and man words. These were newcomers. From Grim's manner and Thorvald's, they seemed important. If they were Elders expecting refreshment, thought Siri, they would have to content themselves with kelp—that is, if the sheep hadn't eaten all of it.

But they didn't look like Elders. Their belted tunics were made of rough homespun. Even at a distance through the rain Siri could tell that it was coarse and plain. Still, as she stretched to peer over the skin boat, she saw long scabbards dangling from their belts. Siri knew that the scabbards contained swords. She had seen some when mariners brought them to Starkland, not to trade to the settlers, since swords were forbidden them, but for protection in distant travels.

Siri gaped at these strangers with swords, who confronted Grim and the Starkland men on the deck. They stood there for a long time. Siri couldn't hear what passed between them. Were the sword-carrying strangers friendly or hostile? Peering through the rain, she wasn't able to tell.

When, finally, they moved toward the middle of the ship, Siri felt a hand grip her shoulder and spin her around. It was the Furfolk man. Releasing her, he reached around and yanked up her hood. She either had forgotten she was exposed or had simply ceased to care. After all, concealment couldn't matter much longer.

Only it seemed to matter to the man. He shoved both Siri and the girl ahead of him and under cover.

Resentful and glum, Siri sank to her knees. At least now she could hear Uncle Thorvald speaking of the bears and praising the Furfolk man who kept them alive. "Sire," Thorvald declared, "the bears still require such knowing care."

One of the strangers replied, "Certainly. This man, Kol, who is underking in the north, will see to these matters until the bears can be moved to the southern realm of my kingdom, perhaps to a forest rich with game near the royal stronghold. For now they will be kept in an ancient fortress not far from here."

"A forest!" echoed Siri under her breath.

She was so thrilled by the thought of the forest that she missed part of Thorvald's response. "And what guarantee do we of Starkland have?" he was asking.

Siri heard a sharp intake of breath. She crept on her hands and knees to peek out at the gathering.

"Do you question my word?" the speaker demanded.

"Sire," Thorvald replied, "it is your father's promise, not yours."

After a long pause the speaker said, "That is so. Still, I am bound by it. Sometimes I am too quick of tongue. The she-bear and her cubs please me more than I have shown. I grow impatient because of urgent dealings far from here. I would have been halfway across my kingdom by now if I had not learned of your coming. But we will feast together and then settle what is owed to you and your men, and to all the banished in the Land of the White Falcons. My sword stands for my word. You may bear it home to your people."

Siri shook her head in disbelief. The king? But he was only a tall man with a red beard and graying hair. What if he was pretending? What if he tricked Thorvald into giving up the bears and then left the Starkland people with nothing? Still, he had mentioned a feast. What would it be like? Grand, if he was truly king. Would they let a child attend? If one child, maybe two?

Glancing back over her shoulder, she grinned at the Fur-folk girl.

20

Before he left the ship, the king wanted to see the Furfolk. Thorvald ducked under the skin boat to fetch the man, who carefully laid aside the bear tooth before stepping outside the shelter.

The king stared. "He is very like a man," he declared in amazement.

"Sire, he is a man," Thorvald replied.

The king shook his head. "Traders from Starkland describe the Furfolk as part people, part animal. We have been told that they stalk their prey on all fours. They den under snow. And they cannot speak like men."

"The Furfolk have a language of their own," Thorvald said.

The king contemplated the bears again. "They say these beasts have a language, too."

Thorvald made no reply.

Still gazing at the bears, the king said, "We have heard that ice bears are fearsome. But this one seems mild."

Thorvald said, "They are clever, powerful hunters. This she-bear has a bellyful of seal. If she were hungry or threatened, she would be dangerous."

The king jumped down to the lower deck for a closer look. The bear growled and nudged her cubs behind her.

"Sire," Thorvald warned, "closeness and staring threaten the ice bear. All the time we held her captive in the village and on the ship, no one was allowed to approach her."

Slowly the king turned and hoisted himself onto the upper deck. For a long moment he regarded the Furfolk man. Then he asked about the children.

"We protect the Furfolk children as we protect the bears," Thorvald told him. "No one has touched them or even approached them."

"I will look upon them," the king declared, "that is all."

Siri clutched herself. Maybe this was the moment Thorvald had been waiting for to reveal her identity.

But Thorvald refused to call out the children. Siri's heart sank. She could tell from his stiff bearing, the reserve in his voice, that he would give nothing away. If she put aside her disguise, Thorvald's deception would be exposed.

"The Furfolk man would regard it as harrying," Thorvald told the king. "He may be slow to anger, but if he considers himself wronged, he is even slower to forgive."

"Tell him I mean no injury to him or his young. Now I will see them."

Thorvald spoke to the Furfolk man, who replied gruffly, briefly, and then fell silent.

The other Starkland men scowled and edged nearer Thorvald, who refused to meet their eyes. "Sire," he said, "the Furfolk man will finish the task he agreed to. He will conduct the she-bear to new quarters and calm her as best he can. He will keep her from killing or maiming those who must learn to tend her. But this can only be accomplished if his ways are respected."

One of the Starkland men spoke up. "We have all passed near the children. There was no trouble. What can be the trouble now that the king has called for them?"

"When the bears are removed from the boat, the man will use the children as he has done before. They will then be visible from a distance. The Furfolk man is unwilling for attention to be paid them. Forcing him can only sow seeds of mistrust that grow bitter roots and deadly blooms."

The king shrugged. "Does he never obey without force?"

Thorvald said, "It is not a matter of obedience. The Furfolk have no ruler. None has the power to banish. He scarcely understood what it meant for us to redeem our freedom. Even though we differ, we have come to rely upon each other. Sometimes we hunt together. The she-bear is his. It is hard for him to part with her, harder still to leave his people and make this journey so that the bear and her cubs might be delivered alive to you. Once long ago I rescued him from the frozen sea. I have told him that with this ice bear he rescues me and all of us in Starkland. This much he understands."

"So," declared the king. "It is not as I thought. How strange," he mused, "that such simple creatures were not overwhelmed at the outset. Your grandparents and great-grandparents carried with them to Starkland things of iron, hammers and axes and knives." He gazed into the faces of each of the Starkland men. "Your forefathers had experience of war. They knew farming and building, mills and looms and ships. In every way they were superior to Furfolk. Even

without swords, surely they could have conquered"—he tilted
his head toward the man—"conquered such as him." The
king shrugged again. "So send him to his lair."

Thorvald flushed, his face set. He uttered a few hoarse
Furfolk words. Siri thought he sounded shamed. The Furfolk
man did not move. Siri guessed this was deliberate. But which
of them refused the king's dismissal, Thorvald or the man?

The king walked back to where his boat was tied to the
ship, his men and those of Starkland in his wake. The Furfolk
man waited for Thorvald to return, and then they spoke
awhile. Siri wished she could ask the girl to tell her what they
were saying, but that was expecting too much.

"There is going to be a feast," she whispered. Instantly
she sensed that the girl was at a loss. Not only was the feast
word new, but so was this phrase for the future.

It was too much to sort out, especially with Thorvald
nearby. Whether or not he had disobeyed the king's command, he was in no mood to tolerate disobedience from her.
"Later," she whispered. Only there she was again, speaking
of the future, plunging the girl into confusion.

Grim stopped outside the shelter. Keeping his voice low,
he urged Thorvald to be careful. "Do not turn the king
against you."

Thorvald muttered something Siri couldn't hear. Then he
added with feeling, "If I am weary of travel, think how this
Furfolk man must long for his home."

"Even so," Grim told him, "Thyrne is where you find
yourselves this day. Heed me, Thorvald. When you meet with
the king again, try courtesy to ease the strain between you."

"Courtesy offered for courtesy given," Thorvald retorted.

"Still," Grim said, "the king is fair. He keeps his father's word. I cannot say the same for some in his service, especially Kol, who is underking. There is scant time before the king departs, but you can remedy this rift."

"His father's word," Thorvald repeated musingly. "And keeps also his grandfather's banishment of our people. Long ago that king took all of one island's goods to fortify his raiders. Loaded his warships with everything, leaving the islanders to undreamed-of hardship. And again the following year, the raiders stopped for the scant harvest. This time the island men set two of the king's ships ablaze and sank a third. So they were seized and all on the island banished. Fair?"

After they walked off, still talking, Siri worked with the girl on the idea of past and future. She remembered that when she had spoken of mother and baby and brother, the girl had seemed to understand that going home would happen. Siri returned to those words, trying to convey the difference between then and now, later and soon. The girl beamed. But Siri couldn't tell whether the thought of mother and baby and brother cheered her or she really understood the lesson.

Two traders returning to the ship were a welcome distraction. One carried a round block of some sort. He was tearing pieces from it and stuffing them in his mouth. "This is what I miss most when we are long at sea," he said to the curious Starkland men. "Here, have some." First one man and then another took a bit, sniffing it before placing it on their tongues. The trader encouraged them. "There's plenty more onshore. Take it with cheese or butter," the trader instructed them. "Wash it down with mead. Ah!" he exclaimed, gobbling more. "There is nothing so good as bread."

The girls were fascinated. Siri longed to taste this new food. Bread.

By now all the Starkland men were examining it, some rolling bits into shapeless lumps, others trying not to choke on it.

"It won't last long in this rain," the trader told them. "Have as much as you like. Give some to the sheep."

Siri prodded the girl. "Go and look. Maybe they'll feed us, too."

Sure enough, it didn't take long before someone noticed the child standing in the rain watching them eat bread. One of the Starkland men tore off a large chunk and tossed it at her feet. The girl stooped to grab it and dashed back inside.

Siri seized it from her. The girl lunged to retrieve it. Crumbs scattered and all but dissolved in wetness. For a moment the two girls glared at each other. Then the Furfolk child divided it.

Siri raised her piece to her nose, inhaling the slightly sour aroma. It was unlike anything she had ever known. She took a small bite and held it in her mouth. She didn't like the way the texture changed. Still, she couldn't resist the taste.

"Good?" she asked. "Good bread?"

"Good bread," the girl echoed in agreement.

When the man came in out of the rain, she presented him with the rest of her portion. He started to eat it, then quickly spit it out, as though suddenly realizing where it came from.

21

All day long people came and went, some trading and some readying the ship for the long return voyage to Starkland and beyond. Even as furs and ivory and fine Starkland homespun were unloaded, goods made of iron were carefully stowed under the deck. Barrels and kegs were exchanged for full ones with fresh cheese and butter and salt meat.

When the sheep were carried off to be traded for two fat ones, Modi from Outermost Farm exclaimed at the uneven dealing. He was told that everyone in Thyrne prized Starkland wool. Siri could almost hear Grandmother scoffing at this. She had always maintained that Starkland cloth was in demand in Thyrne because Starkland women were better spinners and weavers.

Thinking of homespun made Siri wonder where her proper clothing was. Thorvald had better not let it be traded, or she would tell Grandmother. Siri grew indignant at the thought of losing her new shift and coat-dress. If Thorvald challenged her rightful claim, she would whip out the matching cap as proof. And if the clothing had already been sent off the ship, there was bound to be a reckoning when Grandmother learned of Thorvald's misdeed.

Siri still hoped to be included at the feast. But with Thorvald ashore to look over arrangements for the bears, there was nothing she could do but wait. Others wanted to consult him, too. The men grumbled at his long absence. Then someone mentioned that the king had detained him. Siri could tell that this information made them uneasy. By now she was beside herself with impatience and too anxious for lessons or storytelling.

Toward evening the rain let up. But the air stayed dank under dense gray clouds that looked to Siri like mounds of sodden wool. That was just how she herself was beginning to feel: neglected, too long exposed to the uncaring weather.

When a woman and a small child came on board, both girls attached themselves to the slits between the hides and peeped out at the newcomers. The Thyrne woman kept her child firmly in tow until Grim joined them and lifted the little one, a boy, into his arms.

This struck Siri as most strange. Stranger still was the way the woman leaned against him. Surely a man as ugly as Grim was an unlikely husband and father. Yet this was how they appeared.

Siri craned to see some feature of the woman, who was looking at the bears, her back to the shelter. "See the pups," the woman said to the boy.

"Cubs," said Grim. "Let him know them for what they are. This may be our last glimpse of them here, but who knows what beasts await us in our travels?"

Siri kept willing the woman to turn around. But it was only at the last moment, when she smiled up at Grim and the boy, that Siri caught a brief impression of a ruddy face and black, black braids. Siri's mouth fell open. Her hand flew to her head. She longed for a fuller look, but all that was visible now was the woman's shoulder as she stepped out of the way to let a man with a heavy sack edge past her.

"Hair like mine," Siri whispered, thrilled. "Like Siri."

"Like Sister," the girl responded.

After a moment Siri nodded. Of course like Sister, like all Furfolk. But the Furfolk girl had always known others like herself. What made Siri's heart pound and her breath quicken was this discovery that she was not the only odd one. This must be what it felt like to stumble across long-lost kin.

But her elation didn't last. With the departure of Grim and his family and the last remaining men on board, the ship was suddenly left to itself, or to the Furfolk and the bears.

Siri had no way of knowing whether the entire crew was attending the feast. Maybe the traders had their own families to go to. Maybe they had friends to stay with. After all, no one would choose to spend a damp, chill night on the water instead of sitting before a fire and eating hot fish soup and roasted sheep.

At least the girls were able to run about the deck. Such freedom after their long confinement made them silly and wild. Their hilarity brought the man out to quiet them, but then he thought better of this restraint. After speaking to the girl, he led her and Siri down to the enclosure and released the cubs.

Siri understood that they must stay on the lower deck where the she-bear could keep an eye on them. Perhaps because no one else was there, she didn't seem especially anxious. Still, while her cubs chased each other around barrels and tumbled over each other in the sheep bedding, she stood with her muzzle pressed through the wattle as if she, too, yearned to stretch her own limbs and run and pounce.

Long after the cubs were back with their mother and the girls and the man had gone to sleep in the shelter, a rowing boat returned to the ship with some of the men. Clambering aboard and stumbling along the deck, they made much more noise than the girls and the cubs had.

Siri sat bolt upright, wondering what offerings might come her way. Surely Thorvald would have brought back morsels from the feast. Scrambling to the door flap, she tried to sniff the tasty leftovers. But what the men reeked of as they staggered past the shelter wasn't anything she cared to try.

Thorvald came last, with Grim.

"They are too foolish to hear you tonight," Grim said. "Too much mead for those unused to its fire. Tomorrow they will be holding their heads as well as their bellies."

"But the decision must be made at once," Thorvald told him. "We are to bring the bears at daybreak. If not, we had best get under way as quickly as possible."

Siri was bursting to ask what he meant. He sounded as though he might be changing his plan for the bears.

Grim said, "You accepted the king's sword for all the people of Starkland. It is the thing that binds you and the king in agreement. Besides, we are not ready to sail. There are still some crew changes to come, as you know."

"Yes, but we cannot just go forward with this. The men of Starkland have not considered the king's demand, which he made after he handed me his sword."

"And cannot consider until the mead wears off," Grim told him.

"No." Thorvald's voice rose. "They must be roused. Now."

"Has the mead robbed you of your senses as well?" Grim asked. "You could not change the king's mind. What makes you think you can change theirs?" He placed a hand on Thorvald's arm. "At least let them sleep awhile, give their heads a chance to clear."

"And lose any hope of getting away?" Thorvald demanded.

"If you persuade your men to your view, then we will find a way to put off those who expect the bears at daybreak. The move takes place when few are abroad, when there is the least likelihood that something will go awry. You can say the bear is distressed, that she is too unpredictable to take the risk this day. We can sail tomorrow night. We will be far at sea before our absence is noted."

"And if they do not agree—" said Thorvald, but he didn't complete the thought.

After a moment Grim said, "That matter is between you and the others of Starkland. Those of us who sail to far-flung places and risk our lives to trade with all manner of folk must keep our distance from disputes of this kind. We are traders simply."

"I understand," Thorvald murmured. "You have already extended yourself beyond ordinary limits. I will speak with the men when they are able to hear the plain truth."

Truth about what? Siri wanted to ask him. But hearing the anguish in his voice, she knew her uncle too well to think of whispering to him or even signaling him now. Anyway, whatever was tormenting him would be aired soon enough.

She crawled back to her sleeping mat to wait for morning.

22

The Starkland men belched and moaned. They complained that they had eaten something spoiled. It had made their stomachs churn and their heads swell and their eyes burn. What could be so pressing that Thorvald must drag them shivering into the dismal night?

"Day breaks soon," Thorvald told them. "This is the time set for the bears to be taken. Grim will bring the boat and lead the Furfolk man, who will lead the bear."

"And you want us out of the way, as before?" asked Modi, who sounded less churned than the others.

"First we must reconsider," Thorvald said. "Did no one else hear the king?"

Siri was tempted to peek through the slit, but they all were too close. Besides, it was still dark. She would have to imagine how they looked. She listened to some muttering, to more belches and moans.

Thorvald said, "The king expects the Furfolk man to stay with the bears. He claims they are not safely delivered until they reach their final destination. Only the Furfolk man understands the language of the ice bear. So he must keep her for the king."

The men of Starkland muttered some more.

"How can we leave him?" Thorvald demanded.

"Let him think he will be sailing with us," one man suggested.

"Trick him?" Thorvald asked in a voice choked with anger.

"Well, no, Thorvald," another said. "No. Explain that he must remain a little longer, that is all. Then we can send for him."

"Send for him when he is far off in the southern realm of this kingdom, where he will be captive, along with the ice bear?"

"But not ill treated," argued a Starkland man. "The king wants the bear and her cubs to thrive. So he will see to it that the Furfolk thrive as well."

"Hear me," Thorvald said to them, his voice dropping. "The man has family awaiting him in Starkland. There was never any question that he would return with us. What do we gain if our freedom costs this Furfolk man his?"

"Well, Thorvald," said another, "it may not be as we planned. But next to our plight, next to the long, hard banishment of our people, a Furfolk man and his children mean little."

Modi said, "Is that what our Furfolk neighbors will think if we return without the man?"

"It no longer matters what they think," replied the other speaker. "We have no more need of them. From now on we will have swords. We can have their valley and their snow-deer. We can take their land."

Thorvald said, "This Furfolk man is my friend. He has come to our aid. What kind of people betray their friend?"

"Weary people," the first speaker retorted. "Hungry people. People deprived of their rights for five generations and driven to desperate measures. That is who."

A quieter voice intruded. "Thorvald, need we treat the Furfolk captivity as betrayal? Regard it rather as an accident that has befallen us. We accepted the peril of this journey with the ice bears. So did the Furfolk man. That he accepted it because of your friendship makes this outcome bitter for him and for you. I grant you that is a misfortune. Still, we cannot lose for all our people what we have striven to gain. Let the ice bears and the Furfolk be moved."

"And do not betray us," growled the first speaker. "The transfer of the bears must be carried out as planned. If you sow seeds of doubt in the Furfolk man, we could yet be left with nothing. Nothing," he added harshly.

"Enough," said the quieter man. "Thorvald understands what must be done."

Now, thought Siri, Thorvald will tell them no. He will refuse to enter into this plan. But she heard nothing more from him, and by the time the stroke of oars informed her of Grim's arrival, the men had drifted away from the shelter.

While Grim and Thorvald conferred out of earshot, Siri took advantage of the opportunity to find out how much the girl had understood.

"Do you know what will happen?" Siri asked her.

"Bears go land," the girl replied. She smiled. "Father, Sister, Siri go land."

Siri nodded. The girl had not the slightest notion that they were to be abandoned in Thyrne.

But surely Thorvald must be plotting to save them. It will not happen, Siri told herself.

Even when Thorvald called to the Furfolk man and the two spoke, even while Thorvald retreated to the foredeck to give the bear space so that the man could set the ropes, even after the girls had helped him unbind the skin boat and he lowered it over the side, Siri still believed it would not happen.

She tried to stall. "What about these?" she asked the girl, pointing to the tusks and narwhal spiral.

"Bears now," the girl responded with a shrug. And then, grinning, she added, "Tooths later?"

Siri was too distraught to appreciate the girl's attempt to express a future deed.

Just as before, Thorvald assisted the man, each of them standing at opposite sides of the enclosure to hold the bear between them. Near the ship Grim rowed his boat in small circles. Thorvald called to him to move away, to keep a greater distance from the bear for his own safety.

But it will not happen, Siri's mind kept telling her. Thorvald will not allow this. She took the first cub that sauntered over to the gate. It clung to her, as if suddenly alarmed. Maybe she had lifted it too suddenly.

The Furfolk girl got the restless one. Siri climbed onto a keg and from there up to the deck. She managed to keep a grip on her cub while she reached down for the squirming one. The only way she could hold on to both together was to roll onto her back with them on top. They seemed to regard this as a continuation of last evening's play. Siri swung her face from side to side to escape their claws until the man picked one off her and sent his child over the side and into the skin boat to receive it.

Next the man returned to release the she-bear while Siri handed the other cub down to the girl and jumped into the boat after it. The boat rocked dangerously, and water slopped in. That helped distract the cubs and kept them balanced in the center.

As the man stepped into the boat and pushed off, he called to the she-bear. Her dive was spectacular to behold. It took Siri's breath away to see that great, sweeping leap, as joyous as a porpoise arching over the water. The man glanced toward Grim, who began to row away. Then, keeping his eye on the she-bear, the Furfolk man paddled hard.

But where was Thorvald? How could he turn things around if he stayed on the ship? Surely now was the time to halt this course of events, now while the she-bear swam free and the cubs splashed contentedly in the bottom of the skin boat.

Siri gazed at the sleeping harbor. The land rose steeply from the shoreline, the lower houses and outbuildings just starting to emerge through ground mist. She glanced back toward the ship. It seemed a reflection of itself, a ghostly image on the water.

Was Thorvald on his way? Maybe there had been another boat tied to the ship, one she hadn't known about. Or maybe not, since first the bears would have to be set ashore and made safe. Only then would Thorvald be able to rescue the Furfolk.

Grim's boat was turning shoreward. The skin boat followed. The Furfolk child gasped at the sight of a huge structure ahead. Siri gaped. A circular fortress of stone loomed. It was as tall as the tallest iceberg Siri had ever seen.

Grim raised an oar and pointed at a small opening at the base of the structure. The Furfolk man paddled straight toward it, the water lifting the skin boat partway into it and then receding, pulling it out again. Just as the next small wave drove the boat still farther in, the Furfolk man motioned the girls to gather up the cubs and jump out. A wave hit them from behind, knocking them down. One cub, hurled into the water, yelped and paddled seaward. The man shouted something, and the girl flung herself after the cub.

The Furfolk man gestured to Siri. She guessed he wanted her to carry the dripping cub on through the passage. But she kept turning back to look for the girl, afraid that her skin garments would drag her down. "Sister!" she called. "Sister!"

The man had already shoved the skin boat back into open water. She heard him shout again, and then the she-bear filled the entrance.

Siri splashed backward, the cub still in her arms, the she-bear rapidly covering the slight distance between them. Scrambling out of the dark passage and finding herself on solid ground inside a walled yard, Siri let the cub down and ducked into a covered walkway that formed a kind of inner extension to the encircling outer wall. The cub was bleating like a terrified lamb. The she-bear shook herself and then cuffed the cub. She was panting hard.

The Furfolk girl staggered through the passage, the man and the cub that had bolted close behind. The girl was coughing and gasping. The cub, released by the man, galloped up to its twin. The she-bear seemed unaware that one of her babies had been missing.

They all heard a heavy gate slam shut at the outside end of the passage. No one bothered to glance that way. The man held the girl across his knee as water spewed from her mouth.

In the covered walkway Siri held on to the wall with both hands. Still, the solid ground pitched under her feet. Looking down, she could see that nothing moved. Her drenched boots were firmly planted on stone. Yet she couldn't rid herself of the feeling that she was rocked by a powerful sea swell. It made her think of those Starkland men last night, the way they had staggered and stumbled on the deck.

That brought her thoughts back to Thorvald. Was she a fool to believe that he still opposed the men of Starkland? Surely he had only pretended to yield to their arguments.

The ground wouldn't settle beneath her. Even within this massive stonework, nothing seemed to hold her in place. Unsteadily she inched forward and cast her eyes around the open yard at the center of the stronghold. The she-bear was nursing her babies. How clean and white the huge paws were now, paws that enfolded the suckling cubs. The Furfolk man was caring for his child also, pulling off her sopping tunic.

Thorvald cared, too. Didn't he? He wouldn't let this happen.

23

The Furfolk man was daunted by the massive stone that surrounded them. More than daunted, Siri thought. Although the interior wall wasn't solid, the immensity of the entire structure seemed to overwhelm him. He wouldn't leave the central space, the only area open to the sky.

Starting to explore, Siri found that the walkway was divided into separate compartments or connecting rooms that faced the central area. Looking straight across to where the bears rested, Siri could see that above the walkway there was another series of compartments and above those yet one more gallery higher up.

She paused before climbing the narrow, sloping steps that led to the next level. There was nothing to grip, nothing to break her fall if she stumbled. As she stared down at the paving stones, the rocking sensation seized her again. She raised her eyes, forced herself to look ahead, and willed the sea swell gone. Even so, to keep a sense of balance, she brushed against every stone that protruded from the wall.

When she reached the upper gallery, she started out crawling because the floor on this level was scored with breaks and holes, some lightly covered with branches.

Still on her knees, Siri inhaled the pungent fragrance of the boughs. She fingered leaves that were not leaves yet were tender as only living things can be. Something stuck to her skin. Recoiling, she rubbed at the nasty stuff, then found that it bore the same peculiar scent. It made her sneeze, and that made the man call out.

"I'm here," Siri shouted. With the inside half wall for support, she stood up. "Here!" she announced. "Up here! Look at me!"

The man spoke sharply and beckoned to her.

The girl said, "Siri, come, come."

She sighed. "All right," she answered. But she missed the way to the steps. Feeling along the curving gallery, her hands discovered what she wouldn't otherwise have noticed, a huge wooden door set in the outside wall. What was it like on the other side? Did the ground drop away, or was there some kind of outer stairway or ramp? Groping in the dimness, she came upon a chain hanging loose. She used it to pull the door. Nothing gave. She tried to shove it, to shake it. The door didn't budge.

She had to backtrack to find the stairway, and then she continued backing down the steps.

"Wait till you see," she told the girl. She knew this was a boast. She knew the man was so unsettled that it would be a while before he would let either of them out of his sight.

Thorvald might come for them before she had finished exploring. She wanted him to come, but she also wanted to look around some more. "There's a door up there," she said, pointing. "Tell Father. Door."

But the Furfolk man planted himself in front of her, frowned, and shook his head.

"I won't go up again," she said. "Sister tell Father." She gestured to explain, to plead for enough freedom to wander around the ground-level gallery.

After a time the man relented, but he allowed her only limited scope. As the day wore on, Siri tested that limit. But whenever she began to climb, the man's instant command halted her before the girl could summon words that Siri would understand.

Instead, she explored the small rooms with storage closets and niches. She even found salt fish stacked on a stone shelf and brought some out to the Furfolk. "More inside," she said to the girl as the three of them tore into the food. "Siri show Sister?"

The smell of the fish roused the she-bear. She stood up, her nose thrust high. The man threw her a portion, a mere tidbit. She wasn't hungry yet, so she carried it back to her cubs.

The man raised an arm to signify silence.

The first sound Siri could detect as a rattle and scrape came not from the sea passage but from above. Then all at once voices were clearly heard in the upper gallery.

The Furfolk man uttered a single word to the girl, who caught Siri's hand and led her into the corridor underneath and out of sight. The man stood alone.

"Tell the Furfolk we bring food," a man ordered in tones of irritation and contempt.

"I have much to tell him," Thorvald responded. "I will go down."

Siri's heart soared. Thorvald had come. He would not fail the Furfolk.

"No, Thorvald, you will not," declared the irritated man. Then he spoke to someone else. "Take the sack Thorvald carries. And take the bread. Let the Furfolk man see what you are about."

Thorvald said, "Remember, the meat should be hung in an upper gallery where the bear cannot reach it."

"This visit is intended to show the Furfolk who brings food to him and the bears. Now tell him about the well water. Tell him how the waste flows under the stone passage to the sea."

"I did not think I would be kept apart from him," Thorvald declared coldly. "Is this the king's order?"

"I am underking," came the reply.

So this was Kol. Siri hoped Thorvald remembered Grim's warning about him.

"I indulged your wish to come here," Kol continued, "because only you are able to inform the Furfolk about what he needs to know while he and the bears are kept here. There is no telling how long they must bide in the north before they can be brought to the forest. At this moment you can ease his stay while you explain what has befallen him. Let him know that the door to the sea is barred without and that this one lets down to the encircling rampart. The door will be drawn up again when we go from here. Tell him these henchmen will bring food. Then take your leave of him."

A man carried out the Furfolk man's sack and a loaf of bread. Next he shoved aside a cover from the paving.

"Tell him," Kol said, "the man shows him water."

Finally Thorvald began to speak in Furfolk, but so haltingly that he sounded as if he had forgotten the language.

When he faltered, the Furfolk man replied in a long torrent of words. Thorvald broke into that torrent with a statement that sounded like an entreaty. The Furfolk man cut him off with a brief retort. Once again Thorvald spoke, stopping and starting and struggling for Furfolk words.

The girl cried out and then clapped her hand over her mouth. Siri guessed what she had overheard. Thorvald was not telling the Furfolk man where the water was. He was speaking of abandonment. "Mother," the girl whimpered. "Home." Siri pulled her close. No comforting phrases came to her. Nothing could alter the bleak truth. The Furfolk man turned away. He tilted his head as if to fix his gaze on a distant sign far up in the sky.

"You speak of other matters," Kol said. "Tell him what he needs to know of meat and drink, of water and drains."

"He is done with me," Thorvald replied dully. "It does not matter what I say. I am nothing to him now."

Siri was glad she couldn't understand the Furfolk words that Thorvald had used to justify himself and his people. Probably he had offered some lame hope for a future homecoming. She had been spared his feeble excuses, his expressions of sorrow or regret. She could feel herself pull back, detach herself from any feeling that had connected them.

Then, just as she thought she had severed those ties that had kept her from believing the worst of her uncle, she heard him tell Kol that he couldn't leave without his sister's child. After all this? she thought. Did he think he could take her home while he left the Furfolk stranded? Did he expect her to become like him?

"You must think I am a fool," Kol retorted. "There are two Furfolk children. Both remain."

Wearily Thorvald disputed this. "One is not what she appears to be. I am obliged to bring her home."

Obliged. Siri grew rigid, seething at Thorvald's use of her. She would never help him fulfill his obligation to Grandmother, not when it might seem to lessen his failing the Furfolk. Siri had to think of some way to show him that she would not desert her Furfolk sister. But how could she refuse him?

"Siri!" His voice rose. "Step outside. Tell the underking who you are."

Siri clutched her throat. It might as well have been blocked with ice. "Sister," she whispered, "you go. Sister go. Be Siri." It was the only way she could resist his order. "Say 'Siri.' Say 'Uncle Thorvald.' Don't look up at him, though."

Thorvald called again, his voice ragged.

Siri pushed the Furfolk child out of the gallery. The girl took a few steps, then stopped and turned as if she might run back to Siri.

"Say your name," Thorvald directed.

Without making a sound, the girl appealed to Siri, who nodded.

"Speak," bellowed Thorvald.

"Speak," the Furfolk child echoed out of nervousness. "Siri," she mumbled.

"Who calls you?" he demanded. "Who am I?"

"Uncle?" Her voice shook. "Uncle Thorvald."

"There!" Thorvald declared. "Now, pull off your hood. Move back so we can see you from up here."

The girl stood as though rooted. These were too many words, spoken too rapidly, too harshly. She glanced in confusion at Siri, who loosened her own hood and shoved it from her head. "Sister!" she hissed softly. "Like this."

The Furfolk child cast a look over her shoulder toward the man. Siri hissed again. She combed her fingers through her hair, shaking it free.

Slowly the girl unknotted the drawstring of her own hood. When her head was uncovered, she shook it as Siri had done.

The men in the upper gallery were so quiet that Siri began to wonder if her trick had worked. She imagined the men above her leaning out, peering down at the Furfolk child.

Finally Kol spoke. "Enough. I will not be played for a fool." He called the men. "We will conduct Thorvald back to the ship. You can attend to the meat later when I have time to direct you."

Siri held her breath, waiting for Thorvald to react. He might rage at her, but he was also capable of coolly exposing her trickery. Which would it be?

The last thing she expected was utter silence. It was more unnerving than anything he could have done to her. When she realized that he would say no more, she understood that he was defeated. Now she had to struggle to hold on to her anger.

The two men passed close to the girls as they mounted the stone steps and pounded overhead. Still, Thorvald did not speak. Something clanked heavily. There was a grating sound as the door was drawn up. Then came the ring of iron upon iron as the bolt was slammed.

Astonished, Siri let out a long, slow breath of relief. But it was relief empty of triumph and tinged with sadness.

Toward midafternoon the sun finally broke through the cloud cover. It sharpened objects in the courtyard. Here and there paved pathways showed beneath debris. The domed roof of a ruined oven sprawled beside a stone-lined pit, blackened by fires. A great table stone on blocks leaned toward an opening to the channel that sloped to the sea passage.

Siri wanted the Furfolk man to see all this, to begin to take stock of their surroundings. But he stood trancelike, gazing afar.

Although she longed to feel the sun, she sensed that she ought to follow the Furfolk child, who kept inside the ground-level walkway to leave the man as much space as possible. Nor did the bear and her cubs intrude on his solitude. Avoiding the sun, they retreated to the dark recess of the gallery on their side of the courtyard.

Siri showed the girl the steps to the upper gallery, but the Furfolk child was unwilling to stray that far. She kept watching her father as if she expected him to return from his distance to tell her what she must do.

After a while Siri explored on her own. Making her way to the third level, she crawled along the gallery until she came to a slit in the curved outer wall. With her face pressed against the stone, she was able to look through the slit at a narrow corridor of the outside world. She saw part of an earthwork and beyond it a deep ditch and then a section of wall made, not of stone, but of latticed wood.

She moved along the gallery toward other strips of light

from narrow openings. After a time she noticed that the earth rose against part of the outer wall. That must be how Kol and the others entered the fortress. The heavy door in the middle gallery was ground level on the outside. Recoiling from the countless bird droppings that coated everything with a sour-smelling crust, she pushed on toward the next view.

At last she was rewarded, for now she was able to see houses and people and animals. From above they seemed so tiny they looked unreal. Why were the buildings roofed with what looked like precious fodder? Were barn walls really made of sticks and mud? Even some fences were wooden. And what were those spindly posts that branched at the top? They looked something like the contorted stems of dead willow scrub, but the stems were straighter and taller than any plant in Starkland.

At the next chink in the thick outer wall she was able to see part of a green hillside. There under the brow of the hill stood a cluster of posts hooded with a darker, spreading green that formed a kind of roof. Were these trees? If only there were lookout slits from the lower gallery so that she could have a side view of them.

Instead of continuing around, she retraced her steps until she faced the sea. Below her a long shadow stretched from the fortress. Was she standing over the passage? She was unable to see straight down, but it looked as though the tide was out. Was the passage approachable by boat only at high tide?

She pressed so hard against the stone that her face hurt. She was tempted to go on in this direction but stopped at the sound of the door being lowered in the gallery below. She scrambled to rejoin the girl. Only now she was cut off. Whoever had entered the middle gallery stood between her and the courtyard ground.

"Take the meat down to the yard," she heard Kol say.

"Thorvald said it should be kept from the bear," one of the henchmen replied.

Siri crept to the inside half wall so that she could look down into the courtyard.

"I am aware of that. But since the Furfolk man seems not to have moved since this morning, best have the meat near him. Maybe the smell will rouse him."

Siri stared down. After some grunting and grumbling, the two henchmen emerged from the ground gallery with an animal hindquarter.

"That is all," Kol said. "They said that the bear will feed when she is ready, and that may be true of the Furfolk as well. We shall see in a day or two what has been eaten."

As the henchmen made their way back to the gallery, one of them stopped and kicked at the sack that Thorvald had brought from the ship that morning.

"What about this?" he asked. "There might be something of value here."

"That contains his possessions from Starkland," said the other man, walking on.

But the first henchman knelt down and wrenched open the sack. The first thing he pulled out was a bit of worn snowdeer hide. It unrolled, and the carved bear tooth tumbled from it onto the ground. "Treasure!" he exclaimed, picking up the tooth and digging deeper into the sack.

In a flash the girl had darted out from the gallery and

snatched the sack from him. Flinging it out of his reach, she stooped to retrieve the bear tooth. The henchman caught her by the wrists.

From the gallery above Kol shouted, "Cease! Leave her. Leave it."

The Furfolk child tried to twist out of his grasp, but he threw her down, pinning her with his knee.

Kol and the other henchman shouted a warning. Even Siri cried out, not to warn but with the horror of what had been set in motion, for the she-bear charged so swiftly that not even the Furfolk man, waking from his standing sleep, could get there ahead of her.

One moment the henchman was wrestling the Furfolk child, and the next he was hurtling through the air. He landed with a thud against the half wall.

The other henchman, a knife in one hand, a dagger in the other, ran toward the bear as she stood over the child. The Furfolk man moved to intercept him.

"Leave them!" Kol shouted. "If you harm them, you will answer to the king."

The henchman backed away. The bear turned from the child and lumbered over to the man she had felled. She sniffed the motionless body before returning to her cubs, who had just emerged and stood yawning in the sunshine.

"Don't come up here without him," Kol commanded with fury. "Fetch him."

With an anxious glance at the Furfolk man and child, the henchman grabbed the inert man under the arms and dragged him into the gallery.

"Now you know what manner of beasts these are," Kol said.

Siri stared down into the courtyard as she waited for all the scuffling and bumping from below to stop. The Furfolk man seemed dazed, but at least he spoke again. Siri couldn't tell whether he was berating the departed henchman or scolding his child. The girl tried hard to act as though nothing terrible had happened, but she kept gasping as if she couldn't catch her breath.

As soon as Siri heard the door drawn up and bolted, she went down to the middle gallery. There she picked up a sprig of the spiky leaves to take with her to the ground level. She would show it to Sister and pretend it was part of a tree. Maybe when she breathed in its fragrance, a story would spring up to comfort them both, a small, straight tale, spiky and dark, dark green.

24

The Furfolk man remained incurious about the fortress. He merely attended to the ordinary affairs of living. He dragged the hindquarter out of the sun but left it in the ground-level gallery. He tasted the water and then filled a stone basin for the bear. He emptied the sack, handing each girl a snowdeer skin for sleeping. He laid out the tools that Thorvald had packed, including a new knife and some hooks and walrus-hide rope.

Siri tried to explain to the girl that he might be able to use some of these things later on in the forest. It was impossible to tell how much the child understood, although she did say something to her father when Siri finished speaking.

Siri tried with all her might to recall exactly what the king had said about the place for the bears near his stronghold. Would they run free in the forest or would they be confined? How would the Furfolk be kept? Maybe Thorvald had learned more about those arrangements. She wanted to believe that this was why he had provided the new knife and the other things a hunter might use. But it was just as likely that he was merely offering the man these things as tokens of the life that had been taken from him.

As long as the man seemed more himself, the girl was

willing to explore with Siri. Soon she boldly led the way, unafraid to step around gaps in the upper galleries. She gathered eggshells and fish bones to examine later in the light of the courtyard, but she shrank from the views that Siri found so alluring, especially when people could be seen.

Did the girl think that those people were actually as small as they appeared from the highest gallery? Siri started to make up a story about three frost giants in a tower, a man and two children, a she-bear and two cubs. But the girl pressed her finger to Siri's lips and made her stop. After that Siri tried to explain that the people and animals way below only looked tiny. The girl just shook her head and wandered on her own.

Unlike Siri, who recoiled from touching strange objects, the girl burrowed in the dark cells along the gallery and collected all sorts of cups and bowls and a stone lamp without oil.

Siri kept returning to what she could see of the outside world through the narrow openings in the massive wall that surrounded them. She longed to know the names of everything different from home. It seemed to her that if they could be identified, they would somehow become familiar. Maybe then the girl would be able to look upon them.

Later they sat side by side in the sunshine, and Siri began her story about a tree with green feathers. She held up the sprig to show the girl, the bendy needles that grew as close as the teeth on a comb.

"Comb?" asked the Furfolk child.

Siri brushed aside the challenge of yet another new word. She needed to follow this story wherever it led. "Just listen for now," she said. "At the top of the tree perched a green falcon. The falcon could see the whole world, just the way we almost can from this tower. The falcon was the eyes of the tree, but the tree itself had branches that turned into wings, wings as powerful as those of the white falcon, except its feathers were green. And the tree could soar above our heads, free as the air. Only it needed the green falcon to see where it must go."

"Air?" said the girl.

All at once Siri realized how important it was for her to learn the Furfolk language. Thorvald had said that it wasn't based on separate words but on whole pictures. Siri couldn't imagine how a picture could be described without names for everything in it, but she was eager to find out. After all, she was growing used to living with a girl whose name must not be spoken.

"Sister tell Siri story," she said. "Teach Furfolk to Siri."

The girl laughed.

The man, who sat apart from them working on the bear tooth, had listened to the story he couldn't understand. Now he spoke to his child. She replied. He sat for a moment, his hands resting on his knees. Then he resumed his picture-making, the bear tooth in one hand, his old knife gripped almost at its point in the other.

As the afternoon cooled down, the cubs came out to play. The bear, still trailing a rope from her hind leg, ambled into the courtyard and began to sniff restlessly in the direction of the meat. Then she walked over to the spot where the henchman had landed. Siri watched her snuffle around the area, as if to make certain that no trace of him remained.

The Furfolk man rose and went inside the gallery. When

the bear started to follow, he waved her off. She stood there, her head swinging from side to side, until he appeared with a large chunk of meat cut from the hindquarter. He threw it past her toward the part of the gallery where she had slept. She seemed to understand that he was staking out her den area. After that, even when her cubs chased each other all around the courtyard, she kept to that side.

It seemed natural to share the fortress with an ice bear that regarded the Furfolk as part of her family. Siri might not belong in the same way, but she was close enough to have gained some measure of acceptance.

Later, while the Furfolk man and girl ate raw meat, Siri helped herself to bread and salt fish. The girl suddenly changed her mind and made her meal the same as Siri's.

Afterward they washed their hands and faces in the bear water. And when darkness descended, they bedded down in the second level among the fragrant branches, each girl wrapped in a skin but lying close. Because of the immensity of the stone that closed them in, the night seemed darker than the darkest night in Starkland.

They did not close their eyes.

25

When the scraping, clanging sound broke through the dense silence, instantly the girls sat up. But this wasn't the door in the upper gallery. So it had to be the one at the end of the sea passage.

The man could be heard as he moved into the lower gallery. All three waited. Then they heard the murmur and hiss of water. A torch held aloft magnified shadow wings that flickered across the stone.

Thorvald called softly, "Siri!"

"Go to him," Siri whispered to the girl as she followed her down the steps. But what was the point in pretending now? Siri had already succeeded in making her uncle look the fool to Kol.

Then why had Thorvald come back?

"Make haste," he said, coming forward.

The girl stepped out to meet him. As soon as he glanced into her face, he began to speak to her in the Furfolk language.

"Take care," Siri said from inside the gallery. "The bear killed a man who—"

"Do you think it is not known? Word of it has spread to

every person here." Thorvald spoke again in Furfolk. The child replied.

"What are you saying to her?" Siri dermanded.

Thorvald said, "I have told her what I would tell her father if he would hear me. He will have need of me, now especially, since they fear the ice bear. They wanted her bound. I said she would not survive that way so soon after the long journey, after her confinement. Kol is so determined to keep the bears alive that he does not dare ignore my advice. So I will continue to speak for the Furfolk. And I am sending you home."

"No!" cried Siri.

"You will go or break your grandmother's heart."

"I can't leave Sister!" Siri cried.

"You have no choice."

The Furfolk girl retreated into the gallery. She spoke to her father, who ducked down.

Siri tried to summon an argument to send Thorvald away. But all she could think to say was that he would be in trouble when Kol found only one child.

"I am in trouble already," Thorvald said to her. "I will do whatever I can to bring the man and his child home before the men of Starkland raise their swords against the Furfolk and drive them from their hunting grounds. I have told the girl that you and she may not be parted forever, and she has told her father enough, I hope, to keep him from despair. Now come to the boat."

"Will you be with them?" she asked him.

Thorvald shook his head. "I doubt Kol will allow that. But

when he finishes with his anger, he will think how he can use me. No more talk, Siri. We have little time."

Siri stepped closer to the Furfolk. The light from Thorvald's torch barely penetrated the dark, but she could see the man rise and turn to her. He was holding something. He groped for her hand and closed her fingers around the bear tooth. She could feel the incised designs that covered most of its surface.

The girl said, "Father tell story. For Siri for Brother."

"Pictures," Siri murmured. She held the thick, curved tooth up to the light. "Story pictures, for Brother."

The girl nodded.

Thorvald spoke once more in Furfolk. Then he told Siri that if she delayed any longer, she put them all in danger.

What did he mean? What sort of danger? She wanted to challenge him, to refuse to allow his warning to drive her from the girl. But what if this was no empty threat? Her mind raced. If only there was something of herself she could leave behind, something to be a reminder, a promise, a connection.

All at once it came to her that one thing was still truly hers. Clutching the bear tooth, she tugged off the boot that held her long-tailed cap, shook it out, and handed it to the girl.

The Furfolk child seemed to think that Siri only wanted her to hold it. So Siri took it back and then, without dropping the bear tooth, clumsily pulled the cap down onto the girl's head. "For Sister," Siri told her. "Siri gives the cap Grandmother made for Siri to Sister."

The girl's hands flew to her head, feeling the unfamiliar

woven wool. She followed Siri into the courtyard. "Sister give Sister," the Furfolk child said.

Siri turned to face her. "Yes, Siri gives cap to Sister," she answered.

The child tilted her head up to bring her mouth close to Siri's ear. "Sister give Sister," she repeated in a whisper. "Kaila."

Siri went perfectly still as the import of that last word filled her. Kaila. The Furfolk child was giving her name, her whole self, to Siri.

Siri stood there in utter silence until Thorvald grabbed her and propelled her ahead of him down the stone passage, through water, and into the rowing boat.

The light was fitful as Thorvald turned back to slam shut the iron gate. When he clambered into the boat, his torch showed another man, Grim, who rowed them swiftly away from the fortress and then shoreward again.

Running the boat onto the beach, Grim said, "You do not have to do this, Thorvald. You will be an outlaw."

"I think I must," Thorvald replied as he leaped from the boat. He bent forward to shove it off. "Siri's trickery showed me that when all seems finished, there is always something more that can be done." From his stooped position, he glanced up at Siri. "Even if it is only one small act of defiance," he said to her. With a mighty thrust he sent the boat out from the beach.

"Uncle!" Siri called to him, but then she couldn't think of anything to add.

"Tell my mother," he called as Grim's powerful strokes

carried the boat away from the land, "I could not be the hero of our people. I could not bring her the king's sword. Tell her I beg her forgiveness."

The boat dipped and rose and shot through the night, the water shining black, splintered with green and gold.

Crouching low, Siri twisted around so that she could fix her gaze on the torch. It dwindled to a speck before being quenched by the darkness or Thorvald or both at once.

26

When Grim boosted Siri onto the ship, the oarsmen were already in position to row away into the night. All were under orders to keep silent until the ship was clear of the coast.

Without the bears, without the Furfolk and Thorvald, the ship felt strange to Siri. Chilled and dazed, she found herself reaching into the darkness for Kaila. Then she imagined Kaila by herself in the stone fortress, bereft.

Too cold to sleep, Siri listened to the rhythmic strokes of the oars. At last the sail was raised. The men of Starkland, released from silence, boasted among themselves. Along with the king's sword that Thorvald had given up, the ship carried enough iron to forge into weapons for every man in the settlement. Only Modi's voice was absent from this gloating. Siri didn't think anyone cared. The others usually dismissed Modi as a simple youth.

And who was Siri herself now that she was wrenched from Kaila? No longer an unwilling passenger in disguise, Siri was still not what she seemed. Her shadowed self concealed the person she had become. Only Siri knew that she was Sister.

If only she had realized this sooner. If only she and Kaila had been able to find, in the imperfect language they had begun to share, the words that would say, perfectly, what mattered. But that took time, time to overcome the blunders that were bound to rear up before them like icebergs in the fjord, blocking the way to understanding. No words, no time. Instead, at their abrupt parting each had given the other all she had.

Waiting for dawn, Siri traced the markings that covered the bear tooth. Kaila was somewhere in that Furfolk picture story. But Siri knew from earlier glimpses that some images merely suggested what they stood for. Maybe in full light she would recognize Kaila. If not, it would be up to Kaila's brother to pry the story from the tiny incised figures.

Holding the bear tooth up to the milky sky of the new day, Siri studied the markings. One of the images that appeared at first to be an iceberg with a bear and twin cubs upon it suddenly took on a different look. What the Furfolk man had drawn with the tip of his knife was not a bear with a pointed nose but a falcon with its curved beak. And what Siri had assumed were cubs on either side were the falcon's outspread wings.

A falcon on an iceberg! Staring at it made her blood freeze, for she saw the fierce bird as trapped, doomed, like the man himself, like Kaila. If the falcon represented the Furfolk, was this hideous scene what the man intended to show?

Siri made herself examine it again. The fine lines drawn with such care showed the wings raised, lifting the falcon into the air. Siri pressed her fingertip over the image, held her breath a moment, and then cast her eyes on it once more.

There was the hard-edged ice, and here, just taking flight, the upthrust span of wings. It was a vision of freedom, then, and the Furfolk story was not yet finished.

Siri would find a way to say this much to Kaila's brother.